The Dancing Masquerade

The Dancing Masquerade

Femi Abodunrin

DOKUN PUBLISHING HOUSE
IBADAN

Published by

DOKUN PUBLISHING HOUSE
48 Iwo Road
P.O. Box 14552, University of Ibadan P.O.
Ibadan, Nigeria
℡ 02–8104088
E-mail: dokunpub@yahoo.com

First Published 2003

ISBN 978 36937 3 5

Cover:
The Ipada dance in which the masquerade turn his
costume inside out. Costume especially designed by
Georgina Beier for Ojo Ajayi.

Printed by Printmarks Ventures, Ososami, Ibadan

For Ayòolá and Òsúnwèmímó
In memoriam

Contents

UB — So it was a bluff! And the real heroes of the Igbo society are the artists and writers who have been telling everybody that colonialism was just one big bluff!

CA — Yes, and if we win the battle for the minds, the first thing which will go is that rigidity of mind that has come to us with the so-called 'higher religions,' this fanaticism, that can make a man go to war over a matter of belief!

UB — Then you might recreate the spirit of the culture — not by going back to some antiquated custom, but by making people realise again that the world is a market place, which is open to bargain!

CA — Yes and by rediscovering the meaning of the old saying: 'The World is a Dancing Masquerade!'

(From *The World is a Masquerade: A Conversation Between Chinua Achebe and Ulli Beier*)

ILLE

No, not sing,
For those that love the world serve it in action,
Grow rich, popular and full of influence,
And should they paint or write, still it is action:
The struggle of the fly in marmalade.
The rhetorician would deceive his neighbours,
The sentimentalist himself; while art
Is but a vision of reality.
What portion in the world can the artist have
Who has awakened from the common dream
But dissipation and despair?
      (W.E.B. Yeats, *Ego Dominuus Tuus*)

Preface

1. If The Masquerade Dances Well!

Gingerly! Gingerly! Ever-gingerly!
Tenderly! Tenderly! Irreverent tenderliness!
Purposefully! Purposefully! Forever purposeful!
The Masquerade dances — the Masquerade dances well! Ah!
Our masquerade dances well!
The purposeful, ginger, irreverently tender steps of the
masquerade is the Atokun's joy.
Tender steps — I say!
Purposeful steps — I reiterate!
Ginger steps — irreverent to many — but the matter is really
beyond Good and Evil!
Don't stop! Don't look back! Whoever puts his feet to the
dance and looks back is not fit for the kingdom of Arts!
M — as in Movement
M — as in Motion
M — as in Motivation
The three Ms are the hallmark of the masquerade's rhythmic
steps.
Who can stop movement?
Who could hold motion?
Who — I say — can demotivate motivation?
The world — Our world is a dancing masquerade.
Scratch! Pinch! Stab yourself and awake from the slumber of a
lifetime. Watch the redhot blood shoot from your veins to
convince yourself that there is nothing wrong with the
Baluban clime.
Confront frontally...
Attack epistemologically...
Remonstrate with the three Ds of your — our contemporary
existence;
The De-motivation of Motivation
The De-motioning of Motion

The De-familiarisation of Movement.

When the Ds attack the Ms — children of my mother — the result is never stagnation but retardation. Collective retardation fathered collective apathy and collective poverty was born. Poverty of the soul; dissipation of the spirit....

Otherwise why are we not standing still as in stagnation? But backwards — always backwards — as in retardation? Why?

Never mind! Stop listening to these eavesdroppers inhabiting the hothouse of post-imperialist secrecy. They seek to convince you — and I — that the matter is complex — rather too complex to be unravelled in the market place.

Howu! Where else would we take a matter of this simplicity — the Council of Elders or the Stock Exchange?

The gerontological discourse may be more alive today than in ages past — so what? The end of discourse?

But watch — come and watch the Dancing Masquerade.

Co-ordinated — gingerly — tenderly — purposefully!

Confounding — motioningly, motivatingly, movingly!

Ah! This world is a masquerade — a dancing masquerade.

Don't stand in one place — move motivatingly, motioningly to glimpse the Mask.

There is nothing under the Mask? Ask the Atokun. He might show you — ancient one of primordial rememberance.

You're scared of heights? Don't worry — giddiness may show but only for an instant.

> *The dancing steps you took yesterday — Yanke!*
> *Your father musn't hear of it — Yanke!*
> *Your body aches — it aches all over —Yanke!*
> *Curtains!*

2. The Era of Bad-Feeling

Then, hasn't the story been told and must be retold? That long ago — before the saga of the Elesin, and even before we began to blame the gods — children of our mothers — an abomination occurred here. It was what the scarlet did for the perverted souls in our land. It all started with the handkerchiefs — as they say! Like overgrown and pampered

x

children — those we called chiefs urged their own people — 'Go on then, and get scarlet handkerchiefs...and they were captured!'

Simple — essentially simplistic — but true, sadly true. It marks a beginning. The starting point of an ordeal. The origin of a discourse — a discourse, not just in cultural, but also recriminatory signification.

Long before the Elesin capitulated and a very long time indeed before Ojuola's son learnt not/to blame the gods — a monumental incident of conceited avarice occurred here. Those entrusted with the sheer task of procuring antidotes against past recrimination colluded with present malformations and the future was jeopardised. Our future! Again, hasn't it been said and must be reiterated that the elder cannot dwell in the market while a newborn child develops a fractured skull? But that was when elders were elders, and our gerontology was as potent as their attempt to clone their kind.

Ah! The market — the centre of intense activities. A commonplace — open and unprivatised — where the unborn farted and both the ornate and the refined remonstrated with the truculent air. The dead. And what about them? Of course, many are dead who had much say in the matter. But knowing this land warrants that you tread more gingerly than ever — for I am certain you don't want to wake the dead. Or as Omo-Oba says — in those days when men were men many were simply buried alive. We laughed, and sometimes we cried — mortified by the madman's morbid witticism. But there he was utterly unchanging — smote by the rain, bleached by the blazing sun.

Anyway, the gist of this cyclic tale revolves around a journey. And because of a journey — children of our mothers — has the world stopped being a market place? Has our world stopped behaving like a masquerade — A Dancing Masquerade?

Feelings ran high — children of our mothers. Bad-feeling. Insides were filled to the brim. But just as we did with its twin — the era of good-feeling — we invite you to maintain a complex attitude towards this era of bad-feeling. A complex demand to make at a time when feelings are running high —

perhaps higher than ever before!

It was essentially the fault of Lagbaja — elder brother of Ologbeni — who reported seeing the Oluode's dog arrayed in scarlet garment on its way to the market. But then — even though the matter was confirmed by the Iyalode — this matter is — strictly speaking — not about essentialities.

Signification — Capitulation — Bad-feeling — have combined to produce the ensuing tirade. Three factors which in times past ought to — indeed would have stood as the proverbial stones that should ensure that the soup does not spill — alas — served other purposes, and our world was broken — shattered.

As Lagbaja reiterated while reporting the equally complex affair of Oluode's dog to Ologbeni, we have always being signification mad/inclined, but capitulation and badfeeling are two factors entirely new to our body politic. But the era of badfeeling that dethroned the rhetorical era of goodfeeling was also an age when fear ruled men's heart. So, was the case of Oluode's dog, another example of recriminationary signification that characterises the era of badfeeling fathered by capitulation?

Who knows? But what shall we say — children of our mothers — now that historians are confounding philosophers in an orchestrated bid to conflate one era with another? Our vocation — like the healers we happen to be — is to win back the souls — convoluted and confounded — now bearing arms one against another on a matter as complex, and yet as simple as belief! This fanaticism has come to us — by sea and by air — it now permeates the very air we breathe, and men are bearing arms — preparing to go to war over a matter of belief!

But whatever you do, and wherever fate — complex fate — might choose to situate you in this era of our dispersal — our Middle-Passage — while making sense of the ensuing tale — remember — keep it in mind, children of our mothers, that this is no ordinary season of anomie! It is the extraordinary era of badfeeling! Insides are spoilt — many insides would never be the same again. Yet the battle must begin — the battle to win the souls torn to shreds — fallen apart over a question of belief. This is the complexity of avarice — the enigma of feelings — call it what you like, children of my mothers — we have asked for the dark origin of this discourse — shall we not see its discursive bottom?

....

PART ONE

But it was not greed which engendered capitalism and rational production: it was the *disciplining* of greed, its ruthless taming by order and calculation, and its conversion into a curiously disinterested compulsion, indulged for its own sake rather than for its fruits, which really did the trick.

(E. Gellner, *Reason and Culture: The Historic Role of Rationality and Rationalism*)

While reading Proust's manuscript notebooks, I recently noticed the following questions in notebook one, leaf twelve: 'should this be turned into a novel, a philosophical essày?' Knowing how to deal with a topic that preoccupies us... should we treat it *theoretically or fictionally*? Is there a choice? Is it legitimate to favour one procedure over the other?

(Julia Kristeva, *Nations Without Nationalism*)

1. The Great Traditions

It was Iya-Oloka's factory that structured, polished, and refined our first encounter with both deductive and reductive reasoning.

Money in our household was dispensed according to age. From the moment you receive your fair share of what the power-that-be — mainly Baami actually — considers right for your age and stature, you also became, in a manner of speaking, the sole architect of your own fortune or misfortune.

`Armed with our pennies we in turn besiege Iya-oloka's immense factory with consummate and accustomed ease. If the ageless matriarch offended us daily with her major irritant we forgave her daily, or to be more precise swapped our own iconoclastic ranting with hers, as we chanted:

> *Gbegiri lo'ko, amala la'ya*
> *E jeki a yin ponmon logo*
> *Megida inu awa!*[1]

It is extremely foolish to exhaust the entire day's allotment at Iya-Oloka's, but sometimes we did. The three quarters of a mile's walk to school is equally laden with hawkers of various delicacies. Half a penny or so sensibly saved once or twice a week could ensure that you're not reduced to a beggar at Mama Yinka's puff-puff shed just before the railway-crossing, or when it comes to the *kulikuli-alata* of various shapes and sizes at Alubata. *Ago-mokanla,* or eleven o'clock at school itself, was the official break time: here *dodo*[2] *ati rice, asaro-elede* or simply rice served with fish stew reigned supreme. A penny well saved amounted to a sensible stitch in time. At worse you could go a-begging, which wasn't always futile. A scoop of rice here, a slice of fish there and you could count yourself lucky. Win some, lose some is the name of the game. Unfortunately, many among us see themselves as beggars already. It was never easy, these ones will inform you, to procure these pennies from their original and rightful owners — their parents — in the first instance. If you are wise, make a move at once, and seek, as they say, your greener pasture elsewhere. Otherwise the punning pronouncement: 'a beggar can never assist a beggar — terribly sorry!' — could easily become your lot.

But life wasn't all gloom and no fun. At Banana-Bottom, life became a different ball-game altogether. Yes, we jostled for the band-set. Headmaster Titilayo or simply HM as he loves to be called is an enthusiastic drummer. To belong to the band-set is an elitist status. Along with the teachers, you're elevated overnight to the forefront of whatever goes on in the school. At school assemblies, parades through the town, converging at the town centre to welcome an important dignitary, mainly politicians and their counterparts in uniform, passing-by, or even preparing for the youth harvest in our church, your place in the front is guaranteed just by being a member of the band-set.

And very few qualities were needed. You're either a good drummer, a good dancer or singer. Needless to say that for the boys, it was better to drum than dance and they went about it in style. All desks, tables and even concrete surfaces were potential practice grounds. The girls danced themselves lame and voices became hoarse chanting the same songs over and over. The regular ones are those proclaiming us as pupils of a school called St. James's Local Education Authority (L.E.A.) Primary School, who are happy, who are joyous and who learn their lessons in happiness — the song assured every doubter.

None of us bothered to examine the content of these songs. It is enough to be spotted by a teacher as being an enthusiastic singer:

'What-What! What-What! What has Jesus done?'

A question in which we found many answers. For days after it was explained to us, the crucifixion held us spellbound. Velvet voice, Ms. Aina dramatised the gory detail of how the demented mob screamed for Jesus' blood like a living witness to history's classical example of communal injustice, and

3

heightened the tension by bursting into the refrain: 'what-what...!'

It wasn't just difficult but impossible for any of us, *Onigbagbo, Onimole* or *Aborisa*[3] to understand the logic of the mob, and for days verandas of households where tyrants of any shade or colour reigned supreme were treated to mini-concerts that demanded over and over again — What-what? Another leveller it turned out to be as our year in the third grade wore thin, and Ms. Aina prepared us for the end of year annual concert.

HM — Headmaster, His-Majesty, Honourable-Maniac, Holy Moses, *et cetera,* led the parade of stars. He is next in status only to the Education Inspectors that often plague our school. The teachers who followed in varying degrees of seniority had their individual and collective eccentricities and we knew them all.

James Oladapo, six feet and two inches tall, and a pastor's son is the proverbial son of Eli. Ebullient to the core, he is imbued with an un-ending list of allergies. The most disturbing and the one that brings him in constant friction with HM is his allergy to work, especially on raining days. With convincing logic, he argues that all schools ought to be closed during the raining season. After all, as a farming community a lot could be done to improve agricultural output if all we do when there is abundant rainfall is farm. The physician heal thyself aphorism fits him to no end. For Mr Oladapo apparently detests farming. Mr James Oladapo, ex-itinerant performer/dramatist, ex-politician, ex-boxer cum show-promoter: mitigating failures in each of these endeavours led him to teaching and at forty-five one can only surmise that he is truly tired but simply can't afford to retire.

Attracted to the velvet-voice class three mistress, Ms Yetunde Aina, Mr Oladapo has got a formidable rival in Mr Tunde Owoeye. Youthful, exuberant and always impeccably dressed, Mr Owoeye's major failings are his ridiculous grasp of current affairs and a general physiognomy which he would happily exchange for Mr Oladapo's stocky six-two frame. A

4

mathematical wizard, Mr Tunde Owoeye's ultimate ambition is to become an accountant at a time when very few of them in the entire Baluban nation were chartered. He speaks of travelling abroad to achieve his dream as if he has been there already: 'That sort of thing can never happen in England' being the penultimate phrase that ends every decadent behaviour among pupils and teachers alike that deserves a comment from the algebraic adult-prodigy. At thirty-two years of age the sky is the limit for Mr Owoeye's ambition, and in return, Ms Aina appears torn in bits and pieces between falling into the muscular arms of the ex-boxer or settling for a comfortable, but clearly unromantic existence with the future chartered accountant.

The day a fight finally broke-out between Mr Owoeye and Mr Oladapo at a staff meeting, it took the combined effort of Mr Adedigbe and HM to stop the ex-boxer from inflicting irreparable damage on his relatively weaker opponent.

On our part, we took in all the moral and psychological affectations of these masters and mistresses with amused satisfaction:

'Omo-Alufa nearly murdered QED today,' Romoke, a member of the band-set with unlimited access to HM's office reported heartily on our way home.

'Brainless bully!' Motunde hissed.

'But QED must have asked for it.' Laisi, who holds the school record for wearing the ignoble placard 'I AM AN IDIOT' for speaking vernacular, retorted as he began a spirited defence of Mr Oladapo.

Talks of this nature are inadvertently explosive. It could simply lead to a repeat performance of the primordial act of the teachers. Opinions often become polarised along the lines of hatred or likeness for a particular teacher and his/her line of behaviour.

Mr Owoeye, a.k.a. *quod erat demonstrandum* or simply QED, the Latin phrase with which the mathematical wizard concludes his mystifying solution to every complicated equation, is particularly hated for what many consider his egoistic

5

demeanour and arrogance. Mr Oladapo or Omo Alufa, on the other hand, is loved by bullies like himself. The physically weak ones among us needless to say, see the likes of QED or Ms Aina a.k.a velvet voice, as role models.

We were in primary four, and being tutored by Mr Oladapo when Elizabeth Yetunde Ifalowo arrived in our school. Her arrival was purely fortuitous. Her Sergeant-Major father in the Baluban military-police who has been moved from pillar to post during the civil-war was finally transferred back to Aiyeru from where he started. Sergeant Ifalowo's fame preceded his daughter's arrival in our school. The Sergeant is variously described as the no-nonsense driller of all and sundry, including an only daughter who is the recipient of a barrack education that is second to none. Elizabeth's sixth sense about all matters under the sun soon made her the passionately hated daughter of a passionately disliked Sergeant-Major — father by all lovers of indiscipline: *'Iyawo olopa ki bi omo rere, bi ko bi kumo a bi kondo!'*[4] these ones sang. But those who have long sought answers to how to curb abuses of power by local tyrants of all shades and colour found a ready leader in the Sergeant-Major.

The day Elizabeth arrived in our school has since been christened the day of reckoning for one of these tyrants, HM. Officially, school began at seven o'clock. In reality however, HM's macabre show really commences just before the eighth hour. Time enough for any over enthusiastic inspector of education to be led through the first dodgy report about our school, albeit a lesson that never was! But this meant for Sergeant Ifalowo arriving at half past six. To the man of unwavering discipline's morbid consternation, his arrival with his starry-eyed daughter at such an ungodly time for teachers and pupils alike was greeted by the birds and the numerous insects enjoying their well deserved, undisturbed romance with mother-nature before the commencement of the day's stampede by the irate mortals that trample this landscape from 7 am to 2 pm in theory, or 8 to 1 in practice. Twenty precious minutes after the military man has had the entire school to himself and his misty-eyed daughter, HM with an unusual dosage of sadistic procrastination in him arrived.

6

HM is not new to controversy. His entire uncivil administration thrives on ambiguity, unpredictability and controversy, and hardly do we go through a single week without an irate mother, father or both confronting him in the town centre or slobbering across his huge mahogany desk demanding explanation for a child's broken ribs, swollen buttocks, or what have you. But an adversary in full police regalia was literally unknown to Banana-Bottom.

HM alighted from his Raleigh bicycle for the usual ritual of lifting the cycle across the railway crossing. From there it is a mere five-hundred metres to school and the downward slope of the railway embankment means a free ride for the HM and others that ply this route on one extra pair of legs. HM does not have to go far to reach his destination either: stopping two-hundred metres to his office, he sets up camp for the day's latecomers, an ordeal that is without doubt what he enjoys most on the school curriculum. But today somebody else has taken over his command post, as we love to call it. Moreover that somebody was dressed in the ceremonial outfit of the dreaded military-police — kill and go! — as they are also known. The man has probably wrestled rebel soldiers to submission in Aiyerugba or other theatres of a war that is fought so far away from here. If nothing else happened on the day of reckoning but the sight of HM sweating it out under a barrage of question from Sergeant Ifalowo, we would still have returned home happy and fulfilled.

But the scene was much more picturesque. Against the background of our end of the town school with its luxurious green plants and a seemingly endless banana and plantain plantation that earned the school its famous nickname of *Banana-Bottom* stood the Sergeant-Major and his daughter. Pressed back like an army in retreat were over three-hundred pupils, their fourteen teachers, or at least those of them who have arrived. That army in retreat was led by HM.

The rumour-ridden town was agog with the news. Hunters and farmers returning from a whole night's encounter with rodents and jackasses as well as the *itakuns* on their farms respectively, carried news of the barricade on the most effective short-wave radio known to mankind.

Many reported seeing HM on his knees, while others simply reported that the man of war was about to flog the life out of the head-teacher.

Whatever it was was well worth seeing, and latecomers cursed the primordial cause of their lateness. Portmanteaus were abandoned at fish-sellers' for a glorious four hundred and forty yards sprint to the scene of HM's mummification.

It remains highly doubtful if it will be possible ever to separate the facts of the encounter from the fables of the same episode. One thing is clear though, the encounter belongs to the terrain from which myths are made and legends born. In the minds and souls of teachers and pupils in Banana-Bottom, Elizabeth Ifalowo and her soldier father acquired both mythic and fable-like thrust at the same time. Motunde limped to the scene at the tail end of the historic contact as HM made himself clear for the umpteenth time before the one man court of the soldier of fortune:

'I am telling you sir, that school begins at seven-thirty,' HM was saying as Motunde arrived.

'And I am not interested in when school begins, but what preparations are made before then,' the Sergeant replied.

'I can assure you that the recommended time for all pupils to arrive is seven O'clock and the thirty minutes before morning devotion is to enable them clean the compound before learning starts,' HM proffered lengthily.

The military-policeman looked satisfied and the omen of impending holocaust tinged with sadistic aura surrounding teachers and pupils alike was suddenly lifted. Many of us began to count the cost of HM surviving his present ordeal.

'This is my only daughter,' Sergeant Ifalowo stated soberly: 'I have brought her to your school to learn, and by learning I mean moral discipline and academic acquisition in that order. Do I make myself clear?'

'Yes sir,' was HM's candid reply.

A worried glance at his watch showed the small hand moving towards eight, and the big hand on nine. A whole lesson has

8

been jeopardised already, and matters might be worse if an inspector of education should by one last horrific stroke of fate wander into the compound at this historic moment. But riddle me this riddle, the greatest participant in this battle of the titans — fate! — struck again. Lamidi Adedigbe, a.k.a. 'heaven and earth shall pass away,' rode into the school compound on his Raleigh bicycle. Excited by unconfirmed information he had gathered on his way to school, Mr Adedigbe blamed the siege on HM's weak leadership. Dim-witted to say the least, but the class five teacher and leader of a small band of dissidents in HM's cabinet of fourteen proceeded to give a challenge the soldier of fortune expected but did not get from HM.

In a rare moment of articulateness, Mr Adedigbe reduced the already battered HM to rubbles. Allegations, proven and unproved were levelléd at the now mummified 'Honourable Maniac.' From religious intolerance to high handedness during cabinet meetings, Mr Adedigbe rose to pre-eminence. The soldier of fortune swallowed the bait, hook and worm, and awarded the medal of tolerance, endurance and integrity to the most undisciplined member of Banana-Bottom.

Mr Adedigbe's nicotine mutilated incisors shined in the early morning sun like those of the proverbial tiger chanting its tigritude. Mr Adedigbe, chain-smoker, whose other attribute includes a sworn pact with the semi-refined white SM tobacco to which we have heard him time without number, mouth like a would-be groom proclaiming before an unbelieving bride, the sacred refrain 'until death do us part;' and what was more, Mr Adedigbe, sports master, who has led Banana-Bottom's bare and flat-footed football team to one inglorious defeat after the other; Mr Adedigbe, whose rambling defence of his faith ends with palpable quotes from his adversary's penal-code, became in a moment of unforeseen opportunism the hero of Banana-Bottom.

HM did not live to fight another day. The news travelled fast. A visit by a team of inspectors a week after Sergeant Ifalowo's visit confirmed our greatest fear. Incoherent and inarticulate, HM faltered on all fronts. A letter announcing his transfer as Deputy HM to a school at the northern end of

Aiyeru arrived two weeks later.

A cursory search through the panoramic mind of Motunde is the source of the elegy we composed to the fallen head-teacher. Entitled 'Vengeance is mine, says the Lord,' we reminded would-be tyrants of the story of king Saul or HM, and toddling David or Mr Adedigbe, a.k.a. 'heaven and earth shall pass away': and thus the story shall forever be told in Banana-Bottom of how in times past HM slew his thousand, but riddle me this riddle, Adedigbe in astronomical proportion went for the tens of thousands!

The vast undulating terrain known as Banana-Bottom was second home for many members of our household. The vast compound comprises of our church, its chaplaincy, as well as our school. The more you stare at the endless row of banana and plantain plantation, the more you appreciate the appropriateness of the nickname Banana-Bottom or *Idi Ogede* which has since developed into a synonym for our school. The endless row of banana stood regally like structural backup for the church and school. Everywhere we went with our green upon khaki uniform, the chant *'Ti'di bo ogede'* would rent the air. We sang well, but that was all. Neither our football nor relay teams did us any good. Pupils from the other schools with which we competed readily attributed our flat-footedness to our sumptuous consumption of the banana fruit.

We are — as a rule — forbidden to touch any fruit or even go near the plantation.

'Somnolent nonsense,' many of us declared that rule. I mean, what is the point in putting you in a garden, and at the same time forbid you from partaking in the good fruit of the same garden. I mean, God himself did it, and what was the outcome? Regret. And didn't the Bible say in any case that if we are diligent we would eat the good fruit of the land? Of course, we certified ourselves diligent, and without waiting for anyone's approval plunged into the garden. The result was sometimes catastrophic, but what was life without frivolous risks? And Banana-Bottom held many forbidden fruits: mangoes, oranges, tangerines, cashew fruits and nuts, pinkie palm-fruits and nuts — name it, and it was there in our version of the garden of Eden. Every child's innocence was broken the day velvet voice Ms. Aina walked into their class to talk about the Biblical garden, and how the perilous Eve, assisted by that sacrilegious serpent led us out of the garden. The seasonal fluctuations of the fruits ensured that we were in supply of at least one of these fruits at every time of the year. The man we called Ologba — the official gardener, employed by the church and school played the role of the fiery archangel who had the odious task of stopping us from desecrating Banana-Bottom. Blind in one eye and almost lame in one leg, Ologba was least endowed to carry out his task, physically speaking that is. Ologba's inner strength however, always caused us to marvel. He had the uncanny habit of appearing where you don't expect him. Fifteen or even twenty of us could gather around a mango tree, right in the middle of the garden bestowed on us by nature and:

'Did you say that you saw Ologba tending the flowers around the church?' — somebody might ask.

'Yes, I even said greetings, but the rude, blind bat just wouldn't answer. He looked at me with that morbid suspicion of his...' — the other might say.

'Did you pass by his left or right side?' another would chip in: 'Well, if it was by the left, you can forget it, the owl doesn't catch a thing from that angle.'

Ologba had a booming, unmistakably clear voice, and he never moved around the garden without at least one of his disturbingly sharp, glittering machetes. The cutlass was said to be the source of his legendary bravery, and it is said that he can veer into any nook, any cranny of Banana-Bottom even in the dead of night un-perturbed, once armed with any of his favourite machetes. Inside the vast plantation itself, during the day he became the hunter and we were the hunted. When he walks into our midst, like angel Gabriel doing God's work, he goes for the weakest member of the gang — 'bully, sheer bully', somebody might hiss. The practice is as old as creation — go for the weakest member of the pack. The sacrilegious snake did it, and before the twinkle of an eye paradise was lost. I have been caught by Ologba three times already, and to

11

my surprise he simply set me free each time after reminding me of my parents' position in the church: 'Your Uncle is the Secretary of the Church, and your grandmother is the leader of all the women in the Church, and don't you know that we all expect great things from your father when he returns from *ilu-oyinbo*?' 'You won't tell Baami then, that you caught me here?' I would ask. 'Only if you promise me that you won't mix with those friends of yours again.' I promised. I always promise!

It was a long time before we knew that ours was a breakaway church. The founder was a road worker who, as they say, received a distinct call from God to start the church while driving a tractor, and participating with others in the rather complex task of building a network of roads that the newly independent state of Baluba badly needed. History and legend have it that the founder abandoned the tractor straightaway, to the chagrin of his white engineer boss, overseeing the construction of the road. The founder's vision was expansive, and his message veered into the heart, perhaps accidentally, of Baluba's cultural and political dilemma. His years as a road worker, and fruitful interaction with veterans of the second European war of attrition supplied his enormous political insights. The new church that God has asked him to build must be antithetical to the European model. No wonder, I and the other children thought, the white missionaries that toured the schools in Aiyeru visited Banana-Bottom last. Their leader was a frail looking, but surprisingly agile, old white lady. They brought huge piles of glossy magazines, and toured ours and other schools in a shiny white Peugeot 404 kombi. The sight of the automobile, a rare type indeed, sent waves of excitement through all of us, and the piece of news, 'Iya-Ewe is here' was passed around like a deeply guarded secret. Five of our teachers would then join the group of nine missionaries so that the fourteen classes in the school can experience two uninterrupted hours of Bible lessons simultaneously. During these lessons, the trio of Abraham, Sarah and Isaac, the duo Cain and Abel, and the travail of the lone-ranging-Joseph in the hands of his brothers were graphically illustrated on both

12

hands drawn cardboard pictures and glossy magazines brought by the group led by the white missionary, an ageing woman we named rather affectionately, Iya-Ewe. But the most interesting part of the lesson occurred when cartons of powder-milk straight from Europe were distributed in every class at the tail end of the group of missionaries' visit, and that added enormously to the attraction of their visit. Many of us wondered aloud about why the founder had to differ with the white church and as a result make us suffer the agony of having the group visit Banana-Bottom last. The consequence of this doctrinal squabble was there for all to see, we reasoned. While pupils in the other schools went home with an enormous supply of the powdered stuff brought by the group of missionaries, we had to make do with what was left.

The founder, parted ways with the white church because of fundamental differences. It amounts to double speak on the part of the Europeans, the founder and his cohorts reasoned, to condemn every aspect of the Baluban cultural antecedent — be it music, clothing or medicine, not to talk of the thorny issue of one man, one wife, while aspects of European cultural rather than spiritual antecedents were taught as gospel truth. True. But why does everyone, including Mr Owoeye or QED speak about England with such glowing passion? Ever since I knew where they were stranded, I for one — wouldn't know about Motunde — but I am already choked by the constant reminder of the wonder my parents are expected to resemble once they return from *ilu Oyinbo*.

'Well! Well! Well! One thing which you cannot take away from our church is its lively services,' Temidayo, our junior aunt's son, whose father is an ordained pastor in our break-away church reminded us one afternoon on our way home.

'Look, what are lively services compared to the cartons of milk that we're losing to the other schools,' Romoke countered.

'Ah, I can't believe this. So all you care about is milk, haven't you read in the Bible that 'man shall not live by bread alone?' Besides, have you ever been to any of these other churches still following the European model — Oke-Padi — for example?' Temidayo queried.

'What is wrong with Oke-Padi? They look rather orderly to me. And your example just wouldn't hold — we were talking about milk not bread. The difference I suppose is very clear,' Romoke replied, canvassing at the same time for support from the rest of us.

'Now, I can see that you don't know what you're saying. Look they are dead in there — I mean what they call Oke-Padi. Dead as a *dodo*! The white people wouldn't even let them bring a Baluban drum into the place. Just pianos, which are not the only things that are imported, but the organists as well. Look, the founder has freed us from all that,' Temidayo surmised.

'Okay, what about the business of healing without medicine — any medicine, Baluban or European?' I chipped in.

'What about it?' my unrelenting cousin would like to know.

But at the threshing floor, another being of equally demystifying potentiality, adding glamour and if you like, further encapsulating propensity to our household — Baba-elero or Buroda Lamidi equally reposes.

And on the side business that supplements our household's survival, the threshing floor is the centre of diverse activities. Women first grate their fresh cassava before having them milled into semi-fine powder by Buroda Lamidi. These would then be packed into sacks, and heavy stones placed on top of the sacks to ferment the cassava which they'll later dry and fry. Simply fermented and dried cassava met with similar but slightly different fate. The former when fried produces gari for eba or what our eldest cousin Alice, now in secondary school, told us was called student power. Alice's tale of secondary school life after just three months in attendance put innumerable fears in us about the great tradition and the ways every aspect of it has anticipated and positioned itself in different confrontational postures concerning different aspects of the life that awaited us.

If you make it through form one, Alice used to say, the chances are more than ninety-nine percent that you'll make it through the entire secondary school system.

'So what is the make-it rate then?' Ruth asked.

A question that was never answered directly. 'Okay,' Alice would reply, 'take this story about our first week as your example. 'All form one goats this way,' the Labour-prefect shouted. We all went the way he pointed. All of us except the two tallest boys in our class. The prefect, a bully of the highest order grinned knowing that his trap had caught two live goats.'

'So what happened,' Lanre wanted to know.

'The fifth-formers, some of whom were smaller and younger than the two oldest boys in our class took it in turn placing what we call two-dirty-slaps each on the cheeks of the two goats!'

'And how many were they in the fifth-form?' Ruth asked.

'Forty-four. At the end of the week the oldest one packed and simply left the school. The regime had claimed its first victim. And they were not even the school's record holders.'

'Who are they, and what record are they holding?'

'The fifth-formers. Part of the unwritten history of the school which is probably better known than the written ones is the disciplinary methods of the fifth-formers.'

'What then is the record?' Ruth persisted.

'Well, the story is probably ten years old — or more,' Alice said. 'And it concerns a cow who didn't know he was one, also because he was an old one. When the Labour-prefect asked why he wasn't doing what his fellow cows in the first form were doing, he apparently said that he wasn't really supposed to be in form one but it was 'condition' that made him to come to school so late. As you can see yourself, he told the Labour-prefect, I'm much older than you!'

We all roared in spite of ourselves, before Lanre said, 'but the guy was being honest. What is wrong with that?'

'Everything,' Alice replied. 'If you're a cow you remain a cow, and how many rights do you suppose cows have? None. This particular cow, after receiving the mandatory two-dirty-slaps from the Labour-prefect and his fellow fifth-formers, was made to walk on all fours around the compound mooing like the cow he was, with a placard saying 'I am a cow' hung around his neck. He left the College soon after he was released from the punishment, and he was never seen again! From that day every succeeding labour prefect began his speech to every group of first formers personifying the word 'condition'. 'Listen you form one cows, dogs, apes, orang-utans', or whatever caught his fancy, 'I don't know, but really do not care what *condition* has trailed you to your present fate, but it is my job to make your lives as hellish as I possibly can — understand?' to which you're all expected to respond with a resounding — 'Yes Sir!"

'Tell us about student power then,' Lanre said.

Alice had a rueful laugh. 'Student power or *gari* acquires varying degree of pre-eminence, depending on the age of the term.'

'What do you mean the age of the term?'

'Another term for describing the degree of importance of student power. You may be forgiven for mishandling student power at some period when at other times, mishandling may be punishable by death.'

'Death!' Deborah cried.

'Well, only metaphorically. But the junior brother of death is sometimes more severe than death you know!' Alice said in reply.

'Meaning what?' Lanre asked irritably.

'The week of opening or even the first two weeks are called the week(s) of pride. During the weeks of pride, student power is at the background. Everyone knows it's there but no one talks about it. During the week or weeks of pride, tin-fish, bread, chocolate this and that are the orders of the day. But very soon these precious provisions would run out, and this is when student power comes to pre-eminence.'

'And then, what happens?'

'Then the blood-bath begins.'

'What blood-bath?'

'The battle for survival. By the middle of the term the battle has already commenced. Some students come from so far away that they can't even afford to go home for mid-term

16

breaks. They're the ones to watch out for. With their provision exhausted they become worse than scavengers. Soaking, smoking or swimming student-power takes different form. The college record again, belongs to a group of fifth-formers who soaked half a sack of student-power in a drum,' Alice said, pointing at the drum-shaped cylindrical container our household uses to collect rainwater.

'A drum?'

'That was during the week of pride, mind you. Yes, a drum, including twenty-four packets of St. Louis sugar and four dozens of peak milk to accompany it. They called it soaking per excellence.'

'But that's so irresponsible and wasteful,' sanctimonious Ruth said.

'The idea is great,' Lanre yelled. 'What a party it must have been. Was it a great communal party, a carnival, Alice?' he asked.

'It was a party all right. But it also produced the greatest end of term scarcity of student power the school has ever known,' Alice replied sadly.

But at the threshing floor, dried and fermented cassava, are treated with equal, or perhaps greater respect. Like it's slightly more prestigious counterpart beaten from yam into cassava flour and yam flour respectively, the threshing floor is a place of monumental importance. Bantering and unending bantering is the first, the second and the third nature of the threshing floor. And Buroda Lamidi, who lost his entire left leg to an attack of polio at childhood is the life-president of the threshing floor.

Whatever the one-legged man may have lost when he laid utterly supine to the attack of his brand of a particularly acute anterior poliomyelitis, he made up for with his razor-sharp mouth. No housewife in Aiyeru, no matter how foul-mouthed could outtalk Buroda Lamidi. He met them lewdness for lewdness, pouting for pouting. When he sat by any of his grinding machines, with his handsome, lightly cicatrix face, and immaculate uniform you could be forgiven for thinking of him as a recently retired schoolteacher or seasoned administrator. Words like penises or fat, medium, and thin behinds — words that are absolutely taboo in our household acquire commonplace status at the threshing floor. I soon developed the habit of thinking about the place as a separate domain, a different entity or at least a mini-republic. Even Baami never ventured into the threshing floor. His only human contact with Buroda Lamidi is limited to pre-supper time when the man came into the big parlour, washed and dressed in his regular clothes, to give an account of his activities for the day. Despite my love-hate relation with Buroda Lamidi I was the threshing floor president's favourite errand boy. He loved my accurate message bearing/reporting potentialities, and I in turn appreciated his generous tips.

'Look here Lamidi, I haven't come here to flirt with you today, you hear. Just grind my cassava, and let me leave your stinking threshing floor.'

'And have I ever flirted with you? I merely want to take you from your husband — that's all.'

'Who? You?' the woman called Wosila asked indignantly.

'Yes, me — Lamidi! the son of Agbabiaka,' Lamidi replied defiantly.

'Oh! So you're son of Agbabiaka today, and not son of the Imam?'

'Well, I never disown any aspect of my heritage.'

'Well, I guess with you there is no line of demarcation between religion and sacrilege, but that is really none of my business,' Wosila retorted. 'In any case you're too small, *too below*.'

'Where am I too small?' Lamidi asked, standing to his full height.

'There!' Wosila said, pointing between the president's legs. As the other women roared with laughter, Lamidi gave Wosila a sharp crack on her buttocks, simultaneously pulling her to himself: 'Okay lets go and I'll show you. Let two visitors come face to face with each other and we'll see who is small.'

'Hey, Baba-Elero, that's somebody's wife you know?' another woman called Mope chipped in.

18

'Why don't you mind your own blasted business Mopelola. After all, you're just being jealous. How many times have you made passes at me, but I've told you that I really don't like àbùlà!' Lamidi said.

'Hey, see me see scandal O!' — Mope said as she sprang to her feet, clapping her hands several times; 'Would you care to tell all these people the type of *abula* I've ever invited you to?' she asked, trying to free herself from the insinuated scandal.

'No, not the one you mix with your husband's thing, but the real one.'

'Well, I'm sure you're aware Lamidi that one penis or one testicle may be as good as another, but one is always tougher than the other.'

'That's a fat lie Mope. One partridge is never taller than the other, except one is trapped between the ridges and the other stays atop the heap!'

'We shall see today,' Mope retorted. She made a dash for the president's lame foot. The agile president of the threshing floor anticipated her move, did a hundred and eighty degrees on his other foot, and as he came full circle grabbed the woman by the neck as if to support himself from falling. With his secure hold, Buroda Lamidi grabbed Mope's bubbling breast. The woman yelled, and after a mild struggle managed to free herself.

'Worthless man,' Mope spat. 'Just blend my pepper and let me get out of your dirty threshing floor. I don't know how you manage to escape the sanitary inspectors. This place should be closed, if only because of the lewdness of its operator,' Mope rounded.

'Then the whole of your family will simply die of hunger,' Buroda Lamidi who'd returned to his seat replied, simultaneously humming the famous tune directed at sanitary inspectors:

The inspector is here!
The inspector is here!
But I have swept my room
Including my backyard
The inspector is here!

'That's a fat lie, Lamidi. Before corn arrived in this world, hen was not eating cement,' Mope retorted.

Before the president could reply, a chant came from across the footpath: 'Rip the skirt! Remove the pants!' It was Rafiu, a neighbourhood mechanic passing by who hailed Buroda Lamidi from outside the threshing floor.

'Sir Rufi!' Buroda Lamidi called back.

Bedbugs. Lice. Rodents. Three implacable enemies plagued our household. Motunde's fragile frame suffered most. Her suffering might be physical, but mine was mental. For Maami-Agba it was both a physical and a mental agony. She prayed more than ever. That our father and mother may return from the land of their self-imposed exile to find my sister alive.

I was in primary seven and Motunde in six when my sister became terminally ill. We had grown used to many things together. She had her circle of friends and I had mine. Not that she has ever relented — but Maami-Agba prayed more fervently. She hardly slept any longer. Seven and six years respectively since our father and mother departed these shores, and Maami-Agba's one dream was that the pair — who have since fathered and mothered another girl in addition to the boy we named Muyiwa-Oluseyi — would come back and find both me and my sister alive. To Maami-Agba, Motunde's only problem is the constant *Ibá*. Others — less generous attributed my sister's frequent ailment to supernatural causes. To some, she was simply the quintessential *abiku* — and these ones readily cited her glowing beauty, and the possession of a mind that is reputed to function with a preternatural prescience, as proof. She was hardly ever second in her class.

'Tunji, I think we will have to go and see Pastor Gboluwaga in the morning,' Maami-Agba stated matter-of-factly.

'Whatever you say Ma,' I replied, equally confused.

My cousin Temidayo was also awake, and advised that we leave for the church immediately.

'Go and call Folayan for me,' Maami-Agba commanded. She seldom used Baami's first name in addressing him, except when she was herself ill or confused. It gradually dawns on

20

you as you grow that hers was a permanent adjustment to the constantly restructured family tree. Baami was son, husband, father and grandfather all before his time. Temidayo picked his way gingerly across the entangled legs of Ruth, Alice and Deborah still snoring and battling it out on the communal mat.

Soon enough, the frolic sound of Baami's rubber slippers could be heard as he made his way from his abode in the lower part of the storey building through the courtyard and into Maami-Agba's room. Some of the family's nanny goats were inadvertently roused as he and Temidayo disturbed the settled calm of these members of the household during the pre-dawn zone. This part of the household is yet to experience the glow of electric lights like its newer counterpart sitting regally in front. However, every child above the age of five, at which point (officially that is) you're forbidden to wet the communal mat, knows how to pick his or her way to the communal pit-latrine or bathroom both at the back of the oval-shaped six-room house. Of course the wise thing to do is not to run to bed with a water filled tommy, and turn your inside into an arena where morsels of pounded-yam and *osiki* would have to battle it out with *ponmon* and *panla* or strands of *isapa*! One or two hours story-telling sessions after dinner remained the best bowel clearing recipe known to us before bedtime. What was more Àló-Àpamò fostered and sharpened the intellect — along while its twin counterpart, Àlò-Àpagbè — were the best training ground for the aspiring storytellers in our midst. With the roguish tortoise, and the extremely foolish and bullish lion we drew parallels between whimsical and obscene behaviours. The sessions were livelier and more informative still whenever either one or preferably both of the family's disproportionately aged matriarchs could join in.

Baami entered, torchlight in hand. We have never known him to venture into this part of the household without the torch. He knew the pathways like the rest of us, but kept the torch for good measure. When he was in a lighter mood, he might direct the full beam of the torch on any of us, and leave it burning into your face for a few seconds. The playful experiment could also be disastrous, as putting any of us under the spotlight often led to revelation of one closely guarded secret or the other: 'Where did you get that bruise from? Upon discovery you also knew without being told that the day of reckoning won't be tonight but the next morning.

'What is the matter?' — he asked as soon as he came to Maami-Agba's doorstep.

'Folayan, I don't know what else to do about this child.'

'I thought you went to see Pastor Gboluwaga yesterday. What did he say?'

'Folayan, can you go and dress up and follow me to the mission house?'

She has hardly ever spoken to her own son in our presence like that before. Temidayo and I, confused and in profound agony, lowered our eyes unable to look at neither mother nor son. Without a word, Baami turned and went back to his room. Maami-Agba began to dress too: 'I am coming with you,' I said, and without waiting for her reply went out into the darkness to rinse my face and mouth. Maami-Agba picked up Motunde's weak but burgeoning frame, put her on her aged-back, tied a wrapper around her, and used a piece of velvet sash to keep Motunde firmly secured on her back.

Baami was closing the door of the big parlour as we approached his bedroom door. He was dressed and ready. We walked the first quarter of a mile to the church in total silence. The town's hunters were still out. Baami exchanged fraternal greetings with them. It is the height of foolishness to venture out while they are still on patrol; the *ko nile o gbele* or stay in your house *bata* drum is the acknowledged and universal sign that they've taken over the task of securing the town against local as well as external invaders. Their exploits — daring and heroic — are sung in mythical terms and their leader or the Oluode, is a hugely respected citizen. From time to time, the town crier informed the town that daring thieves from Aiyerugba or Aiyederu have written to the Oluode and told him to prepare, on a certain day for an invasion. As a consequence, the stay in your house drum will be heard two hours before its usual time. The heavens help you if you're caught wandering after the drums have sounded. The chant, 'come and buy my *gari oloyo*/won't you buy my *gari oloyo*', in the dead of night tells you that a roaming citizen has been caught,

22

his head clean-shaven, a granite-boulder placed on it and made to repeat this chant throughout the nook and cranny of the town!

We trudged on in silence. Motunde coughed and Maami-Agba slapped her gently on her bottom. As we approached the railway level-crossing, our church, school and the vast undulating terrain known as Banana-Bottom became visible.

A solitary bird perched on the neem tree closest to the railway embankment. It was difficult to ascertain its type in the pre-dawn darkness. Its mournful wailing soon revealed it as *Kowe:*[5] *'Kowe, Kowe, Kowe!* Maami-Agba stiffened. Motunde whimpered.

'Kowe, Kowe, Kowe!' the bird cried again.

'It is a bad-bird Folayan,' Maami-Agba said.

Baami merely stooped, picked up a stone and flung it in the direction of the bird. The stone touched a branch of the tree about the time the bird took off with a final blast of *'Koweeeeeeee!'*

Maami-Agba broke into a gentle sob. 'There is nothing' — Baami said — his voice lacking any conviction.

2. The Dancing Masquerade

One

The moderate heat of the sun presided over a fruitful interaction of disparate aroma. At the northernmost entrance to the vast Owode market, two women argued over the price of a measure of rice, as well as over whether the precious grain the one was about to sell to the other was *aroso* or *ofada*. Corn-cobs littered the ground, and four feet away another streak of haggling between the sellers of roasted and boiled corns and their customers were audible: *ìso-aláso*[6] stood regally, adjacent to those of the handful *aláwo*.[7] Slightly disguised hostility could be discerned by possessors of the proverbial sixth sense, between the various *aládìre* and peddlers of second or only the gods know how many hands clothing otherwise respectfully called *bosikoro or bosi-corner*. The latter, armed with the most famous tool of their trade — tiny clinging bells — created a small band of untrained orchestra giving their part of the market a festive outlook:

> *Bosi-corner ko ye wo!*
> *Ti o ba dara ko san owo!*
> *Ti ko ba dara ko ju sile.*
> *Aloku omo Kora!*[8]

The menu in this part of Owode market is never complete without a mention of its most expensive segment. Here, guinea-brocades, laces and ankara, some as costly as one-guinea per- yard, reigned supreme. The orgy of violence

24

already generated by their presence has since earned their hawkers certain notoriety. The covetous SW, LW, MW and last but not least, FM or Fat Men! that plague Baami's smithy institute are mostly renowned for patronising this section of Owode market. The same orchestra that waxed the latest tune, which many had thought was excellently designed to curb the excesses of the likes of Iya-Sarafa — of the *kini iya aláso nta...*[9] fame — in one quick swoop also remonstrated with what it termed the perverted socio-cultural psyche of those who tend to look with hatred, jealousy or both at the procurers of these obscenely expensive materials.

'Look here my friend, can't you see how they're turning society into a study in contrast?'

'And would you be kind enough to tell me what on earth is wrong with a bit of contrast? The likes of you ought to know that fingers are never equal. Besides, as the famous musician has said, 'don't look at anyone who has the good fortune to clad himself in these materials with envy or hatred — only those who steal deserve to be admonished!' the irritated friend fired back.

We moved swiftly past the tumultuous *iso-aláso*, and for good measure did a volte-face so as to avoid the relative calm of *iso-aláwo* where Maami-Agba had her famous stall.

And there he was, black as soot — stooping in the half-prostrate position we always find him when he isn't hauling mountains of goods from one end of the town to the other — or being taunted by us.

'*Aileru-Kubadi! Afinju alaru to nwo ewu irin!*'[10] we hailed the most reputable load-carrier in the entire town. He may or may not give chase. But it was infinitely more satisfying to us if he did. He remained a derring-do. No one living or dead, in times past or present could match his strength, and in salutation the entire town combined to coin — in salutation to his guts! — the refrain — 'the most famous load-carrier clad in iron.' Unlike Omo-Oba or shadow-boxer, Aileru wasn't mad or any such thing. But buy anything from Oja-Owode — a bag of gari or elubo, and Aileru, famous for his moderate charges, would agree to ferry it to the very end of the town for you.

Times changed, but Aileru resisted change. He fought change. Porters, less powerful, and by far less successful acquired *omolanke* — simplistic wheelbarrows made from plank and powered by a pair of fairly used tyres that any sensible mammy-wagon driver wouldn't dare use again — but Aileru stuck to his gun or his head — to be more precise.

Then one day Aileru overreached himself. A rival porter's futuristic machine or *omolanke* failed him at a most inauspicious moment. The funeral procession was ready, and the glittering casket laid on the *omolanke* when the simplistic machine stalled — 'flat-tyre! the man mused to the unimpressed, rather bemused mourners.

'Go and fetch Aileru,' somebody shouted excitedly.

'Yes, Aileru can carry anything,' another supported. Confusion tinged with excitement broke out within the ranks and file of the mourners. Ten or so minutes later, Aileru emerged and without a word beckoned at the men to lift the casket from the capricious machine onto his head. He took two faltering steps, blinked hard and announced his readiness to accompany the dead man, along with his relatives and friends to the man of the hour's final resting place.

'We are off to Oluyemo,' somebody announced.

'*Kubadi! Afin ju alaru.....*' another half-hailed, but stopped mid-stream as he probably realised the sobriety of the occasion.

'*Yio ba babanla baba e!*'[11] Aileru replied, in complete defiance of the prevailing atmosphere.

'Please, please, we don't want any such language here,' a woman who appeared to be one of the chief mourners complained:

>'*Ile O! Ile O!*'
>'*Ile o l'orun O!*'
>'*Baba re ile re.*'
>'*Ile lo lo tarara!*'[12]

On and on it went. Midway to Oluyemo or Banana-Bottom, Aileru asked that he be given a moment's respite to relieve a urinary urge. The crowd of mourners complied. Four men helped to bring down the casket from Aileru's head, while the motley choir continued its chant, all of them commonplace hymns:

> Mo la ala, mo la ala
> Mo la ala, mo de ade owo
> Mo la ala, mo la ala mo wo ewu oye
> Lojo ti mo ba lo!
> Oke igbala ni ki e gbe mi re. [13]

And much more. Aileru never returned to pick up the casket. He moved swiftly through the bush path which he knew like the back of his hand. Ten, twenty and another five minutes, and the grave realisation dawned on the crowd. The chief porter had abandoned them. In spite of this, Aileru's fame soon spread beyond Aiyeru. He became the subject of fierce speculations. The fact that he failed to make it to the graveside didn't stop many from conferring super-human attributes on Aileru. Wherever he went, we gave chase. Better still if he was heavy laden and couldn't give chase. Then, we merely banter away with the famous porter clad in iron!

Deep inside the market itself, the words on all lips were the same. After their haggling, sellers and customers alike returned to the main issue of the day. Everyone spoke of a town divided into two — or at least, nearly two. In terms of number, one half was by far quite inferior to the other, but probably more deadly.

As ancient worries gave rise to contemporary upheavals, one long dry-season-of-discontent was enthroned instantly in Aiyeru. The heavens themselves, overtly or covertly were part and parcel of the conspiracy.

Alasi is not just a minstrel. From Owode to Idi-Ogun he was a household name. The àgídigbo poet exponent could compose, wax, and craft a song-poem on the most sublime of issues, but his light-heartedness also knew no bounds. Combining the ramifying affectations of all the certified mad of Aiyeru into one poetic exposition, he produced his most famous song to date. Blind in one eye, and semi-blind in the other, no one could cease to wonder how he gathers his biting observations and the acerbic, equally encapsulating songs that often followed.

Yanayo or keep dry and be contented, is a mad woman from the northernmost end of Aiyederu. She wondered into Aiyeru on a hot afternoon during the dry season, and fell in love with the intensity of the blazing sun. Her warped mind led her to believe that Aiyeru was perpetually hot and exotic. She became more excited every waking day. Her sense of the quixotic life of the town and presumed climatic balance led her to establish a permanent abode between Owode market and the railway crossing. On raining and wet days, especially nights, Yanayo's misery was profound. Very soon, she learnt to raid compound after compound where she begged, stole and coveted dry woods that became her exclusive preserves. Drying herself like a wet chicken, and raining thunderous abuses on rainmakers earned her Aiyeru-given name — Yanayo!

Akanji-elo lived in his own house. Apprenticed to a goldsmith in his youth, his love of women, according to legend, led him to his present predicament. His speciality is shifting through every garbage and compost heap in search of — the story goes — a golden apparel he lost ages ago. He was said to have slept with the master's wife and was caught in the act. In anger, his old master placed this curse of shifting through garbage dumps on him:

'Akanji-elo, you killed my child yesterday — kneel down!' — we'll command whenever we encounter him. Without thinking or even taking his eyes off the garbage dump, Akanji-elo will bow slightly by the knees, mumble — 'please don't be angry' — and continue his endless search.

Ewu-iyan or iya-beji is the most violent among all of Aiyeru's mad women or men. Her love of the previous day's pounded-yam was the source of her popular name. Impregnated by the equally deranged Pakata, Ewu-iyan gave birth to her set of twins one night right inside Owode market:

28

'Ewu-iyan gelete!
Omi obe tororo
Su suka ki ngbe ru o
Abori pete bi odo elu!'

was the chant with which we taunted the mad woman into eternal rage.

Alasi's epic composition indubitably put the *àgídìgbo* in the sable hands of Pakata, and the dance-steps in Ewu-iyan's flatulent legs. Yanayo's past, which legend dubbed one of easy life and neon lights in distant, far away Port-city featured prominently in Alasi's song. Yanayo's saga — according to Alasi — revolved around a drink and sleep lifestyle: Guinness in one hand, white SM tobacco in another. In Alasi's creative summation, this is ultimately why Yanayo — like Akanji-elo — is a prisoner of a cultural orgy that you can only emulate at your own eternal peril!

Capitulation, Change, and Chance — in that order — have brought Aiyeru to this sordid state. Procrastination and it's twin ordeal inordinate-ambition, followed very closely. If the world, according to Buroda Tailor, is indeed a Dancing Masquerade, and you can only stand still at your own peril, why — the pro-change elements in Aiyeru wondered — would anyone want to resist change?

The game of chance on the other hand, is as old as the human race. The saga of Osun — the femme terrible in a pack of seven deities encapsulates the phenomenon of chance. But, the danger with Oya reposes in her resilience, and this is why *Oya Is More Dangerous than Sango; The Wife Is More Dangerous Than The Husband!*

But capitulation is the story of laughter — the history of which would be extremely interesting if ever written. Armed with treacherous power — one-half of Aiyeru laughed the other to scorn! This half — insignificant numerically — was backed by power — fraudulent power. You see; *When Two People Laugh At Each Other, It Results in a Quarrel:*

We laugh at those people who laugh at us;
As for those who do not laugh at us,
We never laugh at them;
When two people laugh at each other, it results in a
quarrel.
Ifá divination was performed for Èríntúndé,
Offspring of Èlérìn in the city of Sàjéjé.
He was told to perform sacrifice.
After he performed sacrifice,
He started to triumph over his enemies.
When he became happy,
He said that was exactly what his Ifá priests predicted.

We laugh at those who laugh at us;
As for those who do not laugh at us,
We never laugh at them;
When two people laugh at each other, it results in a
quarrel.
Ifá divination was performed for Èríntúndé,
Offspring of Èlérín in the city of Sàjéjé.
He was told to perform sacrifice because of people who
know one and yet harm one,
Travellers to the city of Ìpo,
Travellers to the city of Òfà,
There is nothing in my own life to be laughed at.

Kajogbola and Okuroro are the night and the day of Aiyeru
respectively. The last time they met, night became day and the
day — not one to be intimidated easily — simply stood still!

But today, the chant, 'Kajogbola has been transformed into
the blazing sun, burning with an apocalyptic intensity,' rented
the air:

Kajogbola do'run O!
O mu janjan!
Onikoyi do'run O!
O mu ranran![14]

30

They would like to capture the *aláséjù*, slice him into bits and pieces, they chanted, so that tomorrow's morsel of cassava flour may flow un-hindered!

But Okuroro, the shortest ancestral mask in the history of Aiyeru, also commands a decent following, albeit before the onset of today's crisis. The emergence of the diminutive Egungun, is forever preceded by a retinue of chanting women proclaiming to the world that they've got a murderer for a husband.

From Oke-Agba to Idi-Ogun is a good mile and a half, and the mid-point between the two is without doubt Oja-Oba. 'The market is our penultimate destination' — both camps chanted — 'market crowd be warned.' Assured that the numerical power of Aiyeru was theirs — that the morality of this struggle was theirs to lose — the lionised and increasingly fanatical followers and supporter of Kajogbola and the Oye-Mayegun camp added the more dreaded addendum:

> *People of the market, clear the way!*
> *We are coming through the market gate*
> *My Lord is coming to the market*
> *My husband, I have arrived*
> *Laroye, I have arrived*
> *Baraye, Baraye, Baraye!*

Heeding the impending apocalypse, Oja-Oba dissolved into many sprawling directions. The power of one who quickly makes himself master of the market place; Esu who buys without paying, and who can cause nothing to be bought or sold at the market until night falls, is too much to risk. Without Esu — as they say — the cosmos would be a battle-field of blind aggression. Now boundaries have been crossed and Esu's presence is not just compulsory, but also altruistic. Leading Kajogbola's dreaded parade was Baba Aderinto — the Esu priest per excellence — the hairtuft of Esu on his head serving as an eternal reminder of whom Orunmila's true friends are. The hairtuft is the telltale sign of the eternal friendship between Esu and Orunmila. And who in his right mind would dare forget the primordial tale — one which occurred the day Orunmila wanted to know who his real

31

friends were. So he pretended he had died. As soon as the deities heard the news they came to Orunmila's house to claim ancient debts. Esu was shaving his head when he heard of Orunmila's death. With a tuft of hair still standing on his head, he rushed to Orunmila's house, tears streaming down his face. Orunmila recognised his only real friend and said 'henceforth — this tuft will remain on your head as a sign of friendship which is genuine!':

> Oju Oja lawa nlo O
> Ero Oja paramo![15]

From the opposite end of Aiyeru, Okuroro emerged from his Idi-Ogun enclave, the retinue of women singing his murderous praises: 'We have got a killer for a husband,' they chanted. The cannibalistic mien of the diminutive masquerade was reinforced by his blood-red-regalia — the matching colour of his eyes — those who were privy to them, readily swore:

> Oloju eyìn
> Abi idodo lomonri![16]

It was sheer coincidence, and one which the opposing camp didn't fail to exploit, that Maron-Feji — for and on behalf of whom Okuroro served as front didn't just hail from Abogunugun — the enclave revered and named after the thousands of vultures that flocked there — and not the cattle ranch that bestowed on the inhabitants of the sprawling compound their historic vocation and identity — but the fact also that Maron-Feji, in terms of physique, was the carbon copy of his rampaging masquerade. The physiognomic analogue turned the Okuroro camp's song of praise into one of derision mouthed heartily by Kajogbola's screeching mob:

> Oloju eyìn
> Abi idodo lomonri!
> Oba malu ni won fi je
> Ile won na nun ni
> Odede won na nun ni
> Ile abere wo bi ile ekute
> Baba won na nun ni
> Omo won na nun ni![17]

Cataclysmic echoes reverberated round the ancient walls of Aiyeru, from Idi-Ogun to Oke-Agba. Never before in the one thousand years history of the town has war cry and internecine strife disturbed the peace of this land so much.

Like all momentous events — the ten-year old strife begged for a logical conclusion. Not that logic — in the true sense the word could have resolved the issues at stake here. In times past and present, the enigmatic WORD tried, but each time it tried, it failed in as many times.

Aiyeru's inhabitant, at home and abroad, could have written with their own blood if and only if this would have given them the resolution they so desired, but one that remained elusive. Before the Europeans departed these shores after nearly two hundred years of colonial plunder, cardinal, among their numerous catastrophic decrees for Baluba and its citizens, was the ordination in Aiyederu of an outpost of treachery comprising of a motley crowd around whom power must repose. Monitored by their mentors and controlled by sheer greed and avarice, the motley crowd swore in return that they would create their kind in their own image. Aiyeru, like the remainder of Baluba ended up with what you will be correct, in theoretical terms, to regard as the proverbial 'two highs' and 'two lows.' The first high, wielders of confounding power, are of the order of European aristocrats — the originators of the colonial enterprise — uncouth, depraved and utterly ruthless! The second high came to Baluba to do the bidding of their masters at home. They arrived as administrators, traders, and as the A.W. Smiths. While the administrators led the frontal, lobotomising attack against Baluba, the traders — a handful, thrived on the principle of divide and rule formulated by the administrators — enthroned the principle of unfair trade otherwise known as corruption — and the Smiths, assisted by the Iya-Ewes began a fierce battle against the spirit and souls of a people!

Because colonial domination is total and tends to oversimplify — very soon it also manages to disrupt in spectacular fashion the cultural life of a conquered people — creating the poor in their own image is second nature to the 'two high orders' in our parenthetical location of 'two highs' and 'two lows.' The first low order is that of our Aiyederu outpost created and controlled by a dastardly combination of the second high order. A cabal, that can be contemptuously ignored in terms of their number, but it is only when you view the colonial enterprise in its imperialistic, cosmic totality that you'll see why our own surprised aristocrats looking at us surprised, are the true negation of national reality; they thrive on new legal relations introduced by the occupying power, by the banishment of the natives and their customs to outlying districts by colonial society, by expropriation, and by the systematic enslaving of men and women.

Aiyeru and her heroic citizens cried a resounding 'NO' to the systematic seduction of the erring one percent of her citizens pitched and locked in mortal battle against the generality of her people, and rejected the accompanying, devil-inspired enslavement of the generality of her men and women.

Only four families in the whole of Aiyeru favoured the wholesale sell-out to the Aiyederu outpost. Hurriedly repatriated from England from where he was said to be perusing the European legal framework and jurisprudence, a burly character called Akinjide, entered Aiyeru one sunny afternoon on horseback. A dastardly crowd paid five shillings each were assembled by the Maron-Feji group to sing the praises of the arriving legal luminary.

Swiftly, the Aiyeru Descendant Union in England dispatched Akinjide's dialectical opposite — an unassuming son of Aiyeru called Ogunbiyi. Apart from Baami's newly acquired mammy-wagon — Ogunbiyi's was the first motor vehicle ever packed in our compound. He brought news of my father and mother — still stranded in white people's land! — and photographs of their now swollen family of four. The girl that came after the boy we named Muyiwa was a replica of Motunde. Maami-Agba promptly named her Adeola, and we agreed that it was a beautiful name. Ogunbiyi held lengthy conversations with Baami on the issue that brought him from so far away. Buroda Taïlor sat absolutely still throughout these conversations in ways that convinced you that the man has already conceded defeat. The issues at stake are now beyond him. The matter has veered into an area he was least endowed to deal with or even comprehend. Ogunbiyi spoke about the Akinjides of Baluba and warned that their mentors abroad have a carefully wrought plan to unleash many of them on the infant Baluban nation. Their number will always be small, Ogunbiyi warned, but their power, because of the backings that would always be accompanying it, will be forever devastating. A cold shiver ran through my spine as my thought veered back to my parents: 'What if my father is like Akinjide?' 'No!' — I cried inside me or so I thought. Baami's heavy voice roused me to life as he asked:

'Tunji, are you alright?'

'I ... I ... I am fine sir' — I stammered, and ran out of the big parlour.

The older peoples' eyes and voices trailed me to the back of our compound, and I heard Baami saying, 'he's the growing lawyer in this house — the exact opposite of his father who is least argumentative!'

But the word 'petition' became the neologism of Aiyeru for months on end:

'We have petísàn the gófúnòr that Maron-Feji must abdicate the throne of Aiyeru without delay.'

'The SMG has been told by lawyer Ogunbiyi that Aiyeru deserves better than the king of cattles imposed on her from the Aiyederu outpost!'

But inside the High Court at the Aiyederu outpost the matter was of a vastly different nature. Ogunbiyi's salient argument focused on number. He played on, invoked and demonstrated the rule of the majority: 'A negligible cabal cannot and must not be allowed to impose its wishes on the vast majority of Aiyeru' — he was said to have postulated. Within minutes of Ogunbiyi's legal submissions Aiyeru was informed of Ogunbiyi's winning tactics and the enigmatic word, DEMOCRACY dethroned the lesser PETÌSÀN as the neologism of an aggrieved people. Sensing defeat, Akinjide resorted to a chain of invectives, and blatant assassination of Ogunbiyi's character and person. In response, the peoples' counsellor — as Ogunbiyi was dubbed — called the invectives a series of 'peculiar mess' to which he declared himself allergic!

Floored by the weight of the evidence before him, served and presented by an eloquent peoples' counsel, the presiding judge, long rumoured to be a sympathiser of the new right-wing elites unleashed on the Baluban state by their mentors abroad capitulated. Ogunbiyi cornered both judge and defence counsel to agree to a popularity test between the two claimants and contestants to the throne of Aiyeru. Sensing defeat, disgrace or both, the pro-Aiyederu group also suffered another crippling setback the day the popularity test formula was drawn out. The leader of one of the four families suddenly remembered his history and recounted it before an open court. Under cross-examination by Ogunbiyi, the leader blatantly refused to acknowledge Maron-Feji as king:

'He was an Adele, and it was the new government that made him a tax-collector! His middle-name is Aroòkàn, meaning he was only thought off! Oye-Mayegun's middle-name on the other hand, is Adegboye, meaning he has arrived to receive the crown — his crown, the leader proffered without being asked.

The proverbial salvo had been fired, and before the open court, the judge, disarmed and frustrated, ruled that two centres, at different ends of Aiyeru be named where supporters of the two contestants would gather simultaneously to help resolve this crisis. The Oye-Mayegun camp chose Ogidiri primary school, while the Maron-Feji camp were asked to gather at the Baptist elementary school.

In carnivalesque propensity, the throng of humanity besieged Ogidiri. A sea of heads turned the Local Education Authority's ground into history's closest accomplice and witness number one of a peoples' wish. Frustrated for ten years, who among the team of monitors from home and abroad would deny their victory:

'Who is saying that we don't have a father?' — they'll like to know.

'*Sege*, we have a father!'

'Oyè-Mayegun is our father!' the others chorused.

Ogunbiyi brought honour and glory to his family. The family's deity Ogun who gave birth to him and gave him his fearless nature was summoned for honour, worship and reverence:

'*Omo ti Ogun ba ti bi,*' — they sang.

'*Ògún ni yio ma je!*'[18] they echoed.

Since every god exists through his/her worshipper — Osunwemimo testifying to the cleansing attributes of Yeye-Osun — according to the non-dogmatic, unritualistic religion of Aiyeru, never interested in the ontological status of gods and spirits! Designed to overcome the distance between man and god, Aiyeru religion has since developed a technique of breaking this distance — if only for brief moments. Through trance, the Sango worshipper could be united with Sango and the Sonponna worshipper became one with Sonponna, and what was more! They could come back from this excursion into the supernatural world with renewed strength, understanding and wisdom.

Ogun, the people of the land declared, lives in everyone who has once been possessed by him. The fierce Orisa of war, who has water but washes with blood — the culture hero; the Orisa who introduced iron, compelling all those who use iron to worship him — warriors, hunters and blacksmiths; restless warrior and true son of Oduduwa, has visited Aiyeru and the inhabitants of Aiyeru prepared to honour both god and acolyte! Ogunbiyi may not want to dwell in Aiyeru, but so what?, many asked. Is that not totally in harmony with the character of the warrior god?, they asked. Go and ask the Onire, and he will remind you of how Ogun first conquered his town, installed his own son as Onire and simply left for further campaigns: 'Covetousness is their problem. Let him go, release him with our prayers. Set the peoples' counsel free, and may he confound all our enemies,' one woman wailed.

'Don't mind them my sister' — another chorused: 'who in his right mind will try to domesticate Osimole? Is he Maami's nanny goat, that they want him tethered like a common local counsellor?'

Bright and early the following morning the new yam was cut in a true and decent Aiyeru fashion at the Idi-Ogun shrine of the deity — the huge yam was severed into two equal halves, neither half surpassing the other, in a single masterful stroke. 'Enjoy the spectacle if you can,' the priest said as his eyes were tightly shut by a piece of white cloth tied round his head:

> *'Laare! Okan ko gbodo ju kan!'*[19] — the deafening
> chant went.

In the full glare of the victorious Alayeru — the people were set free to proceed with the cutting and eating of their own yam. Ogun promptly received the sacrifice of his favourite meat — a huge dog tied to a stick, stretched out and beheaded by a single stroke, with a machete preserved exclusively for this and no other purpose.

Never a sight for the spiritually feeble or sacrilegious powers-that-mustn't-be! Aiyeru religion is realistic about human emotions and instincts, and the sacrifice serves, amongst other things as a discharge of socially dangerous emotions. The tension and concentration of the worshippers mounted incessantly during the lengthy preparations for the sacrifice. Then, as soon as the blood flows, everyone breaks into a relaxed dance. The Alayeru danced back to the palace with the drums saying:

> *Please do not behead me.*
> *I implore you by the king's head.*
> *Do not behead me*
> *As you beheaded Oye and Kitibi.*
> *The warriors have come!*

The carnivalesque climax of joyous celebration witnessed Moremi come up for reference and divine worship: the miraculous corpulence of the Great Mother is celebrated by the voluminous costumes of the Gèlèdé masqueraders — like the ponderous walk of the fat! Or like Orunmila's wife, Odu — the Great Witch! Is it not clear that Oya Is More Dangerous than Sango?

PART TWO

Cultural experience or indeed every cultural form is radically, quintessentially hybrid, and if it has been the practice in the West since Immanuel Kant to isolate cultural and aesthetic realms from the worldly domain, it is now time to rejoin them.

(Edward Said, *Culture and Imperialism*)

Ninety-five percent of my people poor
Ninety-five percent of my people black
Ninety-five percent of my people dead
You have heard it all before O Leviticus, O Jeremiah, O Jean-Paul-Satre

(Edward Kamau Brathwaite, 'Caliban')

3. The Arrivants

One

Then, Maami-Agba's day of glory arrived — the son she has waited for, for the past nine years is due to arrive in two days. In fact the telegram heralding my parents' imminent arrival was sent on the ship bringing them home. A flurry of activities suddenly overtook our entire household. I couldn't understand why all of a sudden everyone was being nice to me. I, Olatunji brother of Motunde the rabble-rouser, the limping bastard and what have you?

In her closet Maami-Agba took me into her bosom — my entire twelve year frame crawled into her aged body as she tried to explain something. Whatever it was, it sounded terrible and I just didn't want to hear. She told me not to worry, that everything would be fine and that I should just understand that the moment she has prayed for, for the past ten years is only forty-eight hours away.

She called her God wonderful, and I was forced to agree with her:

'But Maami' — I asked — 'would I have to go and live with my mother and father?'

'Yes, you can if you like Tunji. Your days of poverty and struggle with the other children for the last morsel in the communal bowls are over at last. God is just wonderful!'

'No, no, no,' I said vehemently. Feeling confused — I blurted, 'No, I don't want to leave you, never!'

We held each other so tight I didn't want to ever let go. Drenched in tears neither of us dared to speak — two people scared silly about a future which for one has clearly entered its twilight days and for the other just starting:

'All I want from you is to prove to your parents that I raised you right,' Maami said at last.

'I will, I will,' I said repeatedly, afraid more than ever to let her down.

We joined the other members of the household in their futile effort to clean up our large compound. In our socio-cultural psyche, England or *Ilu Oyinbo* is a place of utter cleanliness. Tradition has it that the streets are swept daily by special machines and you dare not urinate anywhere. It was from this fairy land that my folks were returning and the more I thought of it the more I was seized by a sense of intense trepidation. Next, it was time to decide who would or would not be going to the wharf — the seaport where my parents, a brother and a sister that I have never seen would be arriving. Naturally, everyone wanted to go, but it was decided that only Baami and I would go. Maami-Agba was excluded because of her age and lack of familiarity with the ways of the city. Maami and the others were advised to wait until the arrivants are able to visit us in Aiyeru.

Of course, travelling the over two-hundred miles from Aiyeru to the seaport in A.A. Labeka's famous mammy-wagon was novelty for me. And finally the sight of the mammoth ship coming to dock created a surge in the crowd. All my mother's relatives were there too, including my maternal grandfather:

'Well, Tunji I certainly hope that you have rehearsed your English, so that you can speak to your brother and sister,' one of my maternal uncles teased.

I smiled, embarrassed in spite of myself. When they finally emerged some thirty minutes after the ship had docked, the sight of the four of them coming towards us was a study in contrast. England must be a very good place and far away too. They have, I was told, travelled on water for more than fifteen days on the fast moving mammoth ship to reach us.

So at last this is the woman who had the effrontery to leave me and my sister when I was barely three years old and Motunde was just one, and the man who left when I wasn't even two — in search of what? Nine and ten years later respectively they come smiling back with two siblings of mine that I have never seen except in photographs and they expect the lot of us to live happily together ever after?

I hated them straightaway. The four of them, and wished they would stop smiling. My father merely touched my head and as I made to prostrate myself everyone laughed. Now, what have I done wrong?

According to my upbringing, don't girls kneel before their elders and boys prostrate? Then I remembered the women missionaries who visited our school in Aiyeru and the way they shook hands with the men — HM and the rest of the teachers. Next, as if she suddenly understood how I thought we were all supposed to behave, the woman whom they called my mother broke into tears.

'That's better,' I thought though my eyes were not even misty.

I looked behind me to see if anything else might have upset her all of a sudden. The blank faces of my paternal uncle and my mother's relatives greeted me, and one of them made things worse by saying to her: 'Mama Femi, its enough!'

I looked once again at myself and the four of them not yet integrated with us. 'Oh!' — I said to myself, 'its the contrast — it must be the contrast.' They looked so clean I was literally scared to touch them. The boy, the older of the two children looked just like myself and very friendly, and I couldn't help but notice that the girl could have been Motunde's reincarnation. The boy smiled at me and I didn't know what to do:

'Mum, is this Tunji?' — he asked in a very strange voice, just like those of the missionaries.

'Yes this is your brother, Femi, and Femi why don't you say hello to Ralph?' my mother replied, drawing me to herself.

What? I almost exploded — I have never even heard the name before. In Aiyeru we called him Oluseyi or Muyiwa! As I was wondering what other shock was waiting for me, the girl spoke in an even stranger voice:

'Mum, is this Baluba?' she asked.

'Yes!' Mum replied again — and went on to say — 'and this

44

is your brother Tunji, my brother, your grandfather......'

As she tried to introduce everyone, the girl pouted:

'Mum, when shall we return to our country? I don't think I could like Baluba.'

That was it! I felt like spanking the life out of her. She noticed my hostility and clung to her mother screaming:

'Tell him to stop looking at me like that!'

'Who?' My mother asked, rather puzzled.

'Tonjey — your son. I don't think he likes me... and I don't like him either' — she replied breathlessly.

'You shouldn't say that. I'm sure he's been looking forward to seeing you' — our mother replied.

In the strange voice I couldn't understand most of what they said. Luckily enough, our parents' accents were not badly affected. What a pity, I thought, to have a brother and a sister speaking just like the group of missionaries that visited Banana-Bottom. I felt a close affinity with my Aiyeru compatriots. If only Motunde was here — or even Romoke, those two would know what to do, I swore under my breath.

Belatedly, my hesitant father moved to hug everyone — his brother, my maternal grandfather and uncles. We all relaxed, and my father advised that we all get something to drink. Suddenly, the arrivants realised how hot it was and began to compare the weather with that of England. From what I could gather, it was like it is forever cold over there. Colder than hale. 'You must be joking,' I almost said when I realised that I was in the midst of adults. I also remembered what Maami-Agba said about letting her down!

Two

The transformation that Maami-Agba had talked about for nearly ten years began faster than I expected. The objects and subjects of my new socio-cultural millieu were stranger than strange. I remembered the tale of the ghoulish gentleman, and the ways Pastor Gboluwaga constantly used that stupefying tale to buttress the biblical injunction — 'not all that glitters is gold!'

Down at the fiery furnace in Aiyeru the analogy of the tale and the injunction held. Baami often held a piece of glittering ornament and by applying a number of goldsmith's logic and their accompanying mumbo-jumbo would declare to the increasingly nervous customer that as glittering as this object is, it's simply not gold. The owner would stare in disbelief, and many would ask if he was really sure of what he was saying. 'Not all that glitters...,' Baami would say. To which his team of ever-growing apprentices would chorus 'is gold!'

At the Palace Hotel where the returnees were accommodated, I went through my first lesson in shock-absorbing. In stark contrast to the scene of utter disgust where Baami and I had spent the night with some distant relatives I'd neither seen nor heard of before, the returnees arrived down at the lagoon slum, life took a completely new turn. Baami only stopped once from the moment we alighted from the mammy-wagon that brought us from Aiyeru to Port-City. As we approached the creeks, he asked for Baba Lati, the cloth-weaver. The man he asked pointed us to a group of shacks, put together as if by the devil himself. Baba Lati hadn't returned, we were told by a rotund woman who appeared to have been pregnant for several years. She greeted Baami warmly and asked after their relatives in Aiyeru. Baami produced a parcel that apparently had been sent by the said relatives. I was relieved to discover that the inside of the house presented some welcome contrast to the house's exterior. Three miniature beds littered the livingroom between which different objects contested other available spaces. A grander version of transistor called gramophone, stood by the window and an object that I was convinced must have been white before but now a shade between brown and red stood next to the gramophone. On top of this object laid hundreds of piles of old newspapers, the majority of which have also lost their original whiteness. Mama Lati went to this object, yanked it open, and produced two bottles of Coca-Cola. Without asking, she opened the two bottles, gave one to Baami and the other to me. For a moment I didn't know what to do. My eyes searched Baami's for clues, and he told me to thank our hostess. I stood up and prostrated to the woman who looked rather surprised. I was embarrassed, but sat down smugly and began to sip the coke. Minutes later Lati came rushing in like a hurricane. He stopped like a mammy-wagon applying full brakes so as to avoid a dog which had surprised it in a flash inches before crashing into Baami. 'How many times would I tell you not to run into the house?' the mother asked. The half-naked lad of about my age stood peering at Baami, and as he lifted his restless eyes, our eyes locked in warm embrace and he nodded at me in a comradely way. Something about him told me I'd seen him before. 'So won't you greet the visitors?', the mother said. 'Welcome,' the boy mouthed nonchalantly. 'Is that how to greet an elder? Hey, the type of children we're producing these days!' Before he could move, Baami drew Lati to himself and patted his head. Within thirty minutes, plates of steeming rice were served with fresh cat-fish, and the rest as they say is history. I must have fallen asleep while Lati was telling me tales of his socio-cultural environment. Hardly anything from my Aiyeru background matched Lati's tales of city life, so I just consigned myself to listening. When I told him that we were in Port-City to welcome my parents, a brother and a sister who were returning from England, Lati sounded surprised.

'So are you going to live with them in Port-City?' Lati asked.

'I really don't know. Such matters are not debated by children where I come from,' I replied.

'Nonsense, where do you come from? Aiyeru, isn't it? Look, I've been there before and I must tell you the place is backward. With your parents coming from England, if I were you, I would insist on living with them here in Port-City. This is really where life is. Even me I can't live anywhere else. And then your parents being from England would probably live in the poshest parts of the city — like Elizabethan Island, or Igbodija.'

I hardly understood a thing of what Lati said, but I said we'll see. I wasn't even sure where my parents were coming from, and the names of the poshest places in Port-City that Lati mouthed merely heightened my nervous condition. I fell asleep while Lati was still raving about Elizabethan Island, but not before he extracted a promise from me to invite him to my parents' would-be mansion once they're installed in it. I dreamt that night that Maami-Agba was dead, and that hers was the greatest funeral Aiyeru had ever seen.

But now the glittering Landrover which had been sent to fetch the returnees from the port drove out just before dark, and all that my frantic effort to catch up with Baami's giant strides made me miss, the day before, came into bold relief. From the back of the Landrover where I sat sandwiched between Baami and my maternal uncles, I caught glimpses of the extraordinary city. Port-City does not tolerate nonsense, I've heard it sung time and time over on transistor. And now I realise why. There are enough vehicles to fill every inch of Aiyeru several times over or so it seemed. Electric poles mushroomed everywhere. Then the stream of people can only be appreciated, I thought, from where I now sat. The network of roads like a spider's web, was to say the least, confounding. How the driver, called Segun, found his way around the myriad of roads remains a misery. He drove endlessly, and I prayed that he would never stop. Lati's talk the previous night flooded my mind, but how to get used to the extraordinary city perplexed me. Then as if reading my thoughts, the woman they call my mother said: 'But Port-City has grown.'

'Ah! you haven't seen anything. When the 4th inland bridge is completed, this city would be something. The growth is unbelievable,' my maternal uncle said.

'But where is all the money coming from?', my mother asked.

'Haven't you heard what the leader said: Baluba's problem is not money but how to spend it,' my uncle replied.

'With all the slums in Port-City, what is he talking about?'

'Ah, that is another matter. Neither he nor members of his family live anywhere near the slum, or even visit them for that matter,' my other uncle said.

'Stop speaking bla-bla, Mum,' the girl called Lizy said. The mother cuddled her instead of clubbing her on the head, as I expected. These kids are spoilt rotten — I thought.

Segun drove into the Palace Hotel at last, as Uncle Sunday commented on Oyinbo children been rather forward and outspoken.

Too forward, I said in my mind, is probably the right term. My mind shifted to the grand hotel and the concept embedded in it. The Palace Hotel. What a presumptuous name, I thought. Who but a king lives in a palace, and is it not said that two kings can never live in one palace? An atmosphere of graft and lasciviousness surrounded the opulent hotel, and its well-appointed grounds.

Three

The era of monumental change or the monumental era of change, if you prefer that — Take Your Choice (TYC) — is most certainly here.

The scourge of returnees amounting to an insignificant one percent of Baluba set about promptly installing themselves at the topmost level of the nation's pyramid of social stratification. The colonial enterprise assumed a new name once the hundreds of dozens of returnees arrived to assume the colonialists' mantle, and they went about it in style. Structures colluded with forms and content could only hide in shock and embarrassment. The logocentric rules of their ideological precursors energized them, and like the proverbial converts, or the inconsolable sympathizer known to be far more piqued than the bereaved, they sang the song of progress in purely technocratic terms, and terminologies.

As I lay on the opulent foam mattress, my body, my being or beingness, as Baami would have put it, ached all over desiring human contact. What began as respect for the communal mat of Aiyeru soon turned into nostalgia for every face, every known heart in Aiyeru. As Baami's dictatorial rule in our household paled into insignificance in the face of the remoteness of the man I was now encouraged to address as Daddy, my heart ached to reach Maami-Agba to let her know about the transformations that have occured in my life — the transformations she had talked about for so long.

Baami left for Aiyeru two days after the returnee's return. He had talked endlessly with my father the previous nights, and as he got ready to depart Port-city they promised to continue their conversations in Aiyeru upon the returnees' impending visit there. Thanksgiving would be at Our Apostolic Church and the Alayeru must be given a free hand in deciding which of the town's many cultural practices would be appropriate in welcoming a deserving son of the soil who has conquered the waves. Call it excitement, over enthusiasm or what have you. But even I was shocked when Baami mouthed the refrain 'afterall no religion can say that we shouldn't appreciate the practices of our forebears!'

But I've never seen very few people occupy so much space in my entire life: Ralph's room, Liz's room, Living-room, Master bedroom and yet there are still more rooms!

Rooms! Rooms! Rooms everywhere and no people to fill them. My mind flew to Lati and his parents' shack at the lagoon and again the contrast was staggering. Almost all of Lati's predictions had come true to the letter, and that frightened me. How could a boy, my own age, predict the life of the returnees so clearly? Elizabethan Island, Lati had said was where my parents would install themselves, side by side with their own kith, and who, I asked myself are really their kins? The world is mixed — that's what the word Aiyeru reiterates — and it was the first sentence ever explained to me as I began to strew words together. But the logic that informed the mixing in Elizabethan Island eluded me. One knew — without being told — that terrible conflicts lay ahead. Discursive and counter-discursive issues needed urgent settlement or at the very least contextualisation, but where do you begin when objects that one side holds sacred are merely art objects to the other side?

Of my two siblings, Ralph was the most tolerant and tolerable — Liz insufferable. Marked resemblance between Liz and Motunde, I constantly assured myself, was the only reason why I've not snuffed the life out of the child prodigy. She knew as much as I did that the ground between us was inherently quaky, and she did her best to steer clear of me. Of course, Ralph exuded major irritants of his own, but not even his worst excesses could match the unending antics of Liz's favourite playmate Michael the destroyer — so named so as to differentiate him from another Michael in the ever-expanding circle of returnees, both young and old.

Elizabethan Island catered for them all. Huge gardens and their accompanying neatly barbed lawns, each tended by a grown man called gardener, reiterated the opulence of each household. A row of duplexes on one side, a second street sporting lines of neatly arrranged bungalows or still more duplexes on the other. The houses were kept so widely apart as if the occupants were aware of one another's reactionary tendencies and tried to avoid each other's eavesdropping company. In spite of this, gossip flowed from compound to compound as the tribe of gardeners intermingled with the hordes of domestic maids, and the retinue of drivers and houseboys — some of whom were older than the masters of the house but were still called boy! This in turn precipitated unending scandals.

Michael the destroyer, whose aggression didn't match his fighting abilities — is a wild cat of about Liz's age. Among Michael the destroyer's two sisters both of whom were left with their paternal grandmother somewhere in Ekitiland while their mother and father like my own parents went in search of the golden fleece, it is Bukola's antics that provided unending amusement for dwellers of Olanibi Street at Elizabethan Island. Very soon, Bukola's tears became as famous as her memorable sayings. The cause or causes of Bukola's tears vary, but a significant half of it has to do with the dietary dictate of Bukola's returnee father, mother, and a brother who was begotten abroad. Give Bukola pounded yam with okro instead of melon soup and the story would end in tears.

'The dish doesn't match the soup,' or vice versa, Bukola would wail endlessly.

The story doesn't end there too, because for Bukola, yam was the source of life and a recourse to cassava in whatever shape or form is either due to chronic poverty or an excruciating lack of imagination, or both. But the returnees' taste buds — as a result of many years of re-acculturation — had acquired diverse habits. With each returning family, cartons of tin food were unloaded out of which a plethora array of dishes were concocted.

'Maami' — as Bukola insisted on calling her mother in spite of the woman's repeated attempt to make her say Mummy — Bukola would say: 'It's only when the dog is away that we go hunting with the sheep. I thought you should know that if you're really my mother.'

52

'I am your mother alright and it's the witch called your father's mother whom I suspect of misbegetting you,' Bukola's equally tough-minded mother would conjecture!

And so the battle raged. Then one day — a day which broke and changed the course of the family's history — Bukola said to her lionised mother: 'You're evading my question again Maami. Monmi didn't beget me. She looked after me and my sister Olu, because you weren't there and it took her combined effort and Olukori's help for her to succeed — or don't you remember again that the long spoon belongs to Kori? You should be grateful to Olukori first and Monmi next, but I've heard you hurl nothing but insults at the two.

'Well you see Bukola, I am a Christian, and that fact alone rules out thanking or even acknowledging Olukori as you call it. And as for your father's mother, as I've told you she's a witch. If only you know what I've suffered in the hands of that woman.'

'But the woman you call a witch is the leader of the women in our Church — do you say that merely because you don't like her?' Bukola — who already stood on equal terms with her mother in terms of physique — often asked.

'Watch how you talk to me young lady. Don't forget that I'm your mother. Yes, I don't like your father's mother, because she has never liked me. And how do you call someone a Christian who mixes respect for God with the worship of idols?'

'We would have to separate the two matters then,' Bukola responded.

'What two matters? Look, I'm not going to stand here all day and argue with you. You eat what is put on the table or you go hungry.'

'I don't mind being hungry, Maami,' Bukola said coolly. 'This land and its people taxed themselves so hard to send you and others like you to go and learn about the white man's power — his secrets — and not to go and become white yourselves. We thought you were going to return with the theories and practices of liberation and not icons of further colonisation and enslavement!'

The crack on Bukola's face could have shaken the earth. But to all consternation and amazement, Bukola took the mother's slap without blinking. The tearful girl whose tears filled buckets over pounded-yam and melon soup not even wincing at the sound of a perfectly delivered, well aimed slap. Incredible. An inward rather than outward strength no one thought existed suddenly manifesting, making her look incredibly beautiful.

'Don't talk to me like that you daughter of a wicked witch.'

'Which witch?' Bukola queried.

'Your father's mother — she is the witch.'

'But I'm not her daughter. I'm your daughter. That means you're the witch.'

Bukola's mother was incensed. Her beautiful face contorted and her shapely mouth twisted into a serpentine curl.

'Oh, so I'm now the witch. It's certainly true what they say that if the farmer is slow in reprimanding the thief, there's nothing stopping the thief from turning round to call the farmer a thief.'

'And whose saying is that, Maami?'

'A human saying.'

'I am glad you're now tapping into humanity's collective storehouse of knowledge and wisdom instead of the mono-lithic after-thoughts of the land of your sojourn. Yes, Maami you're still one of us. That is one of the wisest sayings of our people — If the farmer is slow in apprehending the thief, it is in the nature of thieves to turn round and accuse the farmer,' Bukola said, breathlessly reappropriating her mother's rheto-rical lines.

You've got to be accustomed to mechanical images to appreciate what happened next between Bukola and her mother. Erstwhile concealed and unshed tears flowed freely on both sides of Bukola's smooth cheeks. Her lips trembled as she placed shaky fingers on them to muffle smiles of joy threatening to turn into roaring laughter. Bukola looked at her mother anew — repeating loving entreaties without uttering a single word. In contrast, age, wisdom and experience featured on Bukola's mother's diminutive demeanour and a thin line, like a fading furrow between two heaps of mound, appeared on the mother's forehead. Weariness displaced tiredness and truth prevailed. Bukola took two faltering steps inside the large living-room and stopped as if uncertain. Bukola's tears flowed freely and it was the mother who reasserted control over a precarious situation.

'Come here! You daughter of Olatosa,' the mother said.

'Maami! *Omo amufa se mogun se! Ari baba mogun jo!* You're the true daughter of your father.'

Bukola's mother laughed mirthlessly, blinked hard in an unsuccessful attempt to stop three solitary flashing drops of tears.

'Get the hell out here Olatunji. This is no sight for sacrilegious souls,' Bukola commanded without even looking at me.

I scrambled to my feet only to fall back into the extra cushioned couch, but scrambled back and stood there like a stupefied chick immobilized and transfixed by the mesmerising hawk displaying its cannibalistic hawkitude. My only path out of the large living-room blocked by Bukola's mother's half-naked brown back. Without turning, Bukola's mother said in a voice I don't think neither I nor Bukola have ever heard before:

'I'm sorry I ever fought you — both of you. Tunji and Bukola there is nothing wrong with your upbringing. We're the ones trying to be what we cannot be. But the story is far more complex than you can both imagine. By picking huge holes in every aspect of the univocality of The Great Tradition, you've managed to poke the darkest origins of a very deep matter. And whoever does that must be shown the discursive bottom of the matter because as our people say, half a reptile does not inhabit the bosom of mother-earth. How we arrived singing songs of enslavement and further colonisation is no simple matter. But when you've been lobotomised, there is no easy way out of your socio-cultural dilemma. Your choices are few and limited, and you simply become a mere passenger in the saga of your own undoing. The surgical incision has to be reversed and that is what has happened here today. You see, we think in one language and express ourselves in another language — indeed we struggle to express ourselves in another language. How can whatever we utter make any sense even to ourselves? The colonial enterprise becomes doubly dangerous when you've been released but you can never habour the thought of releasing yourself. The reasons why this is so is again very complex. Majority of us even transcended the initial lobotomy administered by the colonialists themselves. We took out plastic surgeries of our own — surgery to the tongue — so that we can sound more and more like the colonizers. Hell! Imagine a thirty year old screaming dementedly, 'I want to be white! Make me white, when she or he has for three long decades walked the earth with this tough hide tested and seasoned by the blazing sun? Knowing that the market existed, a whole tribe of Chemists were manufactured to produce bleaching creams. Oh! Isn't the result utterly laughable? I have a friend who has a whole trunk box full of wigs of diverse shapes and colours. Skin bleached white, she's the only black human being I know who sleeps with blue eyes! 'If my house catches fire, I've heard her say many times, 'I'll go straight for my box of wigs and make-up before saving my own soul!'

Bukola said with trembling voice: 'Maami don't you think you should stop now,' and the fear in her voice was plain. Is this the same girl whom the mere sight of coarse cassava flour or gari induced buckets full of tear? Often screaming, 'It chokes the throat! It chokes the throat! Oh, it's utterly strangulating Maami?' I wondered. The Ekiti girl had by now totally disappeared. The Bukola who sang the praise-name of yam — chanting:

Yam! Yam! Yam!
You're of the purest whiteness
You have a gown of meat
You have a cap of vegetables
You have trousers of fish
Yam! O Yam! O Yam!

The mother smiled, drew Bukola to herself and beckoned at me to come closer. I moved sheepishly forward and my right knee kicked a stool knocking it noiselessly onto the carpeted living-room floor.

56

'Well, how can you understand what you've just done,' Bukola's mother said. 'Sit down Tunji and let me talk to you. I don't know what to make of today, but it would rank as one of the greatest days in my life, a day I conquered fear — fear of who I am. And who would have guessed that it would be children like you who would lead me into a new life. As my grandfather of blessed memory used to say, 'When I tell you that it is water that would cook the hardest rock into tender softness, you just ask me for the ashes!" Bukola's mother laughed in spite of herself.

'You just take a look at the stable societies of the world. I mean societies really uncontaminated by any form of colonial intervention or enslavement, not to speak of their twin-evil neocolonialism, and the arguments against colonialism would begin to speak for themselves. Some of the societies I'm talking about exist right there on the European continent, so the evidence is incontrovertible. Take a typical one, right there at the edge of the Baltic sea — one of the most homogeneous countries in the world — which in the exact words of one of its bright minds possesses 'an unbroken history of self-government since our beginning (apart from the second world war), constitutional change at a comfortable speed since the Vikings, a shared and unthreatened language despite our small number (just over five million), a national literature, enough won and lost wars to create enough national monuments, and a state religion, shared by virtually everybody. This uniformity was only broken by those whom we colonised and treated as second class citizens but they remained mainly on the piece of land we gave them and were not incorporated into the society...' Bukola's mother read as she set down the cyclostyled article in her hand.

'Now tell me, how did this society develop as a mini-European state — a power by its own right — except by being left alone and allowed to exist in a state of sheer complementarity with the rest of the world through its homogeneous language, State literature and religion — all giving her the much needed opportunity to uphold her own comprehensive world of myth, history, and mores — a total context within which this world like any other 'world' is unique? The moment that complementarity is lost, whether in hermeneutics or epistemological pursuits don't we have the inalienable right — God-given, Sango-stricken, I don't care! — but don't we have the right to suspect an abandonment of what one of our own founding fathers has rightly described as 'this simple route to a common humanity? It sounds so simple doesn't it? Oh! How succinctly simple, we've obfuscated it. Sickening!'

'The pursuance of the alternative route as our father said, for whatever motives — underline his words WHATEVER MOTIVES! — can only amount to a dastardly attempt to perpetuate the eternal subjugation of our people.'

The logicality of her claims and the vehement passion with which they're delivered left Bukola and I so numb we could only stare. In the end it was Bukola who asked the quintessential question.

'Maami,' Bukola said in a very tender voice. It was as if she was addressing and simultaneously acknowledging the woman as her mother for the first time. The effect wasn't lost on Bukola's mother who shut her eyes tightly.

'Since when have you known all this, Maami?' Bukola asked.

'Always,' Bukola's mother replied without thinking.

'But, but — why —?' Bukola stammered.

'Why all the fuss? Why all the pretences. Why? Why and why? Well, Bukola the answer is quite simple. Our ancestors knew that the world in which we live is a Dancing Masquerade. I mean, the world is like a dancing masquerade — if you want to see it you don't stand in one place. It's very much like the Annunciation of the gospel — In the Beginning What Was? Age-old question that has energized many egos, and dwarfed giant sensibilities — but does it really matter what was in the beginning? An individual response or theory would suffice. Who doesn't need a beginning — indeed who doesn't deserve one? Or to put it in another way who could be without one and live? Whether at an individual or at the level of the collective — what matters is that your beginning must be yours and not somebody else's. It's as I said, first and foremost, an individual question and it is a point of locomotion and not automation — see? But treated as the latter, rather

58

than the former, it's also a question capable of dooming an entire people into a standstill — an epistemological and hermeneutical standstill. Look at it properly and you'll see why and how we have moved without moving. We have seen without seeing! Oh! how I hate opportunistic puns! she cried — 'but is it not true that we have equally heard without hearing?"

'Ask all these returnees from the lands of our subjugation about the many uncomfortable moments in the processes of acculturation in their different fields — and I mean from Philology to Atomic Physics. I know that ours is a collective failure, but let no one tell me that I didn't try. I moved from Philosophy to Literature and back to Philosophy before settling for Social Anthropology. Immanuel Kants's *Foundations of the Metaphysics of Morals*, not to mention how I am, I mean how we're handled in Hegelian dialectics cured me of my philosophical illusions, and D.H. Lawrence, among others, ended my incursion into literature as abruptly as it begun.'

'But National Consciousness, as another founder warned, has got its fundamental pitfalls, and this you've got to keep track of. Awareness of who you're and the son or daughter of whom you happen to be must always be coterminous with a clear awareness of who your neighbour happens to be. 'And who is my neighbour? Whoever I've got the ability to help — not in the vulgar material sense of today, but in the quiet and seemingly unpersuasive way you kids have gone about things around here. Mind you, the dog which is destined to get lost never hears, I prefer listens, to the hunter's whistle! You remind me Bukola of my grandfather, the great Osanyin priest of Ekiti — *Omo amufa se, mogun se* — as you rightly summoned him. And you Olatunji has always impressed me as a reincarnation of some Magba Sango.'

'Then why does Maami-Agba in Aiyeru liken me to a lawyer, and not the priest-ancestors you say I resemble?,' I asked feeling tight within me. Bukola's mother laughed mirthlessly again.

'Probably because you're argumentative. But the real truth is probably because your grandmother like the rest of us is running away from something — the something we all fear —

our past. It's all so silly really, but that is it. Your grandmother, that tall, calm and dignified woman has been thoroughly harrassed by life. Have you ever been told of her suffering during the *lukuluku* epidemic?'

'I have,' I replied but the woman carried on as if I hadn't spoken.

'Three sets of healthy twins wiped out just like that, and she wasn't alone. It was a societal rather than an individual catastrophy. The gods were livid and they had a right to be. Here was a culture preaching nothing but tolerance and respect lying supine simply because another tradition — Great Carthaginian — as we called it — had just arrived which you ought to welcome and respect, but whose colonising spirit should be contained at all cost.'

'But Maami,' Bukola interjected. 'You've got to help me with something there. Why then was it possible for Babalola's holy water to achieve so much, if as you said it was the gods that were angry with the people?'

'The answer is simple really. Well, I should say I've got a theory rather than an answer,' Bukola's mother said. 'And theory for me is just a framework — a possibility — rather than the smart talking it has become today. At its inception — all Babalola's revival meetings did was calm people down. It pulled a multitude away from the uproar which their lives had become. If you remember the central theme of Babalola's crusade — it was called 'healing without medicine' — any kind of medicine — native, foreign or what have you. In the process, it achieved two miracles without fighting a war — holy or unholy. First, it stopped the nativity drugs in their stride while exposing simultaneously the hollowness of the foreign laboratories. The gods must have been pleased with Babalola and his followers.'

'Excuse me, but that is blasphemy. I mean, how can pagan gods be pleased with the Christian God for usurping their roles? Praises for the cure or miracles as you call it were given and delivered to Jesus of Nazareth and not Sango of Ilubu, Ogun Onire or Osun Osogbo? I don't see...'

'Tunji, what you should understand is that neither Sango nor Ogun or Osun are essentially interested in praises. Not

60

even the Jesus of Faith — who must be differentiated from the Jesus of History — exists solely because of anyone's praise or the lack of it. Strange?'

'Not really. I just haven't looked at it that way before.' I replied still thinking.

'Okay, take even the most critical fallacy of them all — Esu-Elegbara, Satan and the Devil. Where do they meet? Nowhere. Esu is not Satan in the same way as Satan is Lucifer or the Devil in Christian liturgy. Let me read you a joke,' Bukola's mother said as she walked to the neatly arranged giant book shelf across the living-room, taking out an edition of *The New Left Review* from the second row:

'A joke has been going the rounds in theological circles for some time now,' she read. 'It goes like this. The Pope was told by the Cardinals that the remains of Jesus had been dug up in Palestine. There was no room for doubt: all the archeologists, scholars and experts were agreed. Teaching about the resurrection, the lynch-pin of orthodox Christian faith lay in ruins. The Pope sat with his head in his hand, pondering his position and that of the Church he headed. He decided it would be only decent — whether or not it would be Christian no longer seemed to matter — to let the separated brethren know. So he called up Paul Tillich, the leading Protestant theologian, and told him the sad news. There was a long silence at the end of the phone. Finally, Tillich said: 'So you mean to say he existed after all...!'

Bukola and I exploded with laughter. 'Well, you see, Esu could have spun that joke and that is his role. To help you and I guard against complacency which is what we've sunk into right now. The question remains between the Pope and Paul Tillich who is the better Christian?'

'Tillich,' I said.

'Neither,' Bukola countered.

'Okay, I said the other time that it was D.H. Lawrence and others like him who ended my literary career even before it started. Now let me explain what I meant. Lawrence went on all his life castigating what he called 'the ugly imperialism of any absolute. Now this is a man whose defense of the novelistic genre alone is couched in absolutes! 'I don't believe in any dazzling revelation, or in any supreme Word, Lawrence wrote. 'The grass withereth, the flower fadeth, but the Word of the Lord shall stand forever. That's the kind of stuff we've drugged ourselves with. As a matter of fact, the grass withereth, but comes up all the greener for that reason, after the rains. The flower fadeth, and therefore the bud opens. But the Word of the Lord, being man uttered and a mere vibration on the other, becomes staler, more and more boring, till at last we turn a deaf ear and it ceases to exist, far more finally than any withered grass. It's grass that renews its youth like the eagle, not any Word, Lawrence concluded. Now, here is a man whose ancestors trampled every inch of this universe conquering, enslaving, colonising! luxuriating and carrying on an eternal battle between withering grass and the Word — living or dead! By the time I picked up his *Sons and Lovers*, I could only cry louder and louder 'Bull to an hostile class of teachers and colleagues, and the entire romantic creed — so I just had to quit. And now to think that a whole generation of Balubans have been trained to think and write like Lawrence becomes the most upsetting fact of all. And you can only cry, where for Christ sake is Esu?'

Four

Bukola was installed at Queen's, and I headed for King's school. Like the proverbial signifiers they'd construed themselves to be, the denizens of Elizabethan Island considered the education of their siblings to be of uppermost importance. St. Claire's would not do for Bukola, just as Malosa Boys didn't appeal to my own parents. Arguments for and against our nativity vis-à-vis the more modern outlook that these schools peddled in varying degrees played prominent roles in the choice of schools. One school had too many locally trained staff, and was therefore disqualified, while the other was chosen for having a large number of foreign-trained tutors or even headed by an expatriate.

But we prattled and fretted. Months after the returnees' return the inhabitants of Aiyeru waited for a visit from them in vain. As a result of the hectic life of Port City in general, and the cosy ones of Elizabethan Island in particular, the land of my birth began to pale into insignificance, and I was alarmed. Then one day Baami appeared without warning. The returnees were first alarmed, then irritated.

'But Buroda you should have warned us that you were coming,' my father finally said to his elder brother.

'Nonsense,' the older brother spat, his own irritation and anger barely concealed. 'After all the discussions we had here before I returned to Aiyeru the last time, one would have thought that you would have visited us by now,' Baami concluded.

My mother and father as excuses cited pressure of work and the ever-growing traffic of Port City, but Baami wasn't impressed. The preparation for the returnees' visit, he declared was of supreme importance, and the occasion had been postponed twice to the chagrin of neighbours and well-wishers, and the shame of the family. Indeed, Baami had come with an ultimatum from Maami-Agba — or so it seemed

— that stated clearly that if the returnees are not in Aiyeru within the next two weeks, they shouldn't bother to visit the land of our birth again. I was bemused when later that evening Baami commented on the changes that have occurred in my own demeanour within the first year of the returnees' return.

'We call him the Alayeru here in Elizabethan Island,' my mother said, 'and you wait until you've met his alter-ego. They're as raw as each other.'

'And who would that be?' Baami asked.

'Oh, the daughter of one of our friends. The parents left her with her grandparents in Ekiti, just as we left Tunji with you in Aiyeru. The two have become the barometers with which we measure several things on this island,' my father proffered.

His brother looked baffled. Worry and incomprehension was written all over his cicatriced face: 'As long as they can defend and uphold the logic of their upbringing,' he said at last.

'Defend?' my father nearly screamed. 'These kids can do more than that. As Mama Tunji said, they're the barometers with which we measure several things here. Through them we know how spoilt our other children are, and they remind us of tastes that we shouldn't have acquired.'

Baami looked pleased finally. He handed his *agbádá* to me just as he would have done in the big parlour at Aiyeru. But instead of hanging the garment on the door, as I would have done in Aiyeru, I took a wooden hanger, and hung it on the rack provided for just that purpose in front of the living-room. It was Baami's turn to be bemused, and a sardonic smile played at the corners of his mouth.

But the visit to Aiyeru, when it came, proved to be a communal affair — as Aiyeru came together to welcome a son long lost to the outside world. The motorcade was stopped twice at the outskirts of Aiyeru. The retinue of dancers led by Maami-kekere were bent on extracting whatever was extractable from the returnees. Aiyeru was in a festive mood and from the back of the Landrover where I sat huddled between my maternal aunt and another distant cousin of my mother I could see just that!

We've been expecting you!
Welcome! We hope you have travelled well!

The talking drums wailed. Aiyeru's advancement — indeed the ancient town's arrival on the world stage was proclaimed, and every citizen felt that she or he had a share in the returnees' accomplishments — whatever those were.

The fountain-head of that arrival was attributed openly to the view of the world — upheld since its foundation — by the town's founding fathers.

'Aiyeru — the world is mixed! The world is a dancing masquerade — if you want to see it you mustn't stand in one place!' the laconic towncrier wailed. Praise names collided with reductionistic hyperboles and the rest, as they say, is history.

At the first stop the motorcade was halted by the advancing party of Maami-kekere and her group. She ordered my father out of the glittering Peugeot 404 in which he sat ahead of motorcade comprising of four Landrovers bringing our family friends from Port-city. Maami-kekere's face was an epitome of concentration. She knelt by the open door of the car and opened ceremonially the water jar she'd held close to her bosom, *inter alia*. A younger woman knelt beside her and proceeds to remove my father's shoes. Maami-kekere rolled my father's trousers above his knuckles and began to wash his feet:

The dry leaf would forever float on water
Just as the osi-bata must reign atop the river
You will prevail above all your enemies!

The women she led roared in the affirmative, Amen! Only then was the man of the hour made to touch the soil of Aiyeru for the first time with his bare feet:

We've been expecting you!
Welcome! We hope you have travelled well!

The talking drums echoed again. The Eesa — second ranking chief to the Alayeru led my father to a white stallion sent by the Alayeru to convey a deserving son-of-the-soil to his palace.

65

Before climbing onto the horse, the Eesa produced a garment complete with an *abeti-aja* and proceeded to drape my father in them. The king's *kàkàkí* sounded to the accompaniment of *bata* and talking drums. Once on top of the white horse — the burgeoning crowd roared — with the knowledge that Aiyeru would spare nothing in welcoming, indeed reclaiming her son:

> *The world is mixed!*
> *The world is a dancing masquerade —*
> *If you want to see it you mustn't stand in one place!'*

The laconic towncrier wailed again. The dirge composed by an unknown mother extolling the virtues of the school system was sung by another group of women:

> *If and when I beget a child and*
> *She or he grows up!*
> *I will definitely send her or him to school!*

Majority of the crowd had waited in and around the Oba's palace. The pomp — not to mention the pageantry — set to climax the day had been reserved for this centre of intense activity. Oja-oba or the king's market is just such a centre. At the entrance to the Alayeru's palace — the ageing Eesa who had walked beside the stallion on which my father rode advanced forward to prepare for the mock battle with the Alayeru — but the second ranking Esu priestess signalled them to a halt:

> *Laroye!*
> *Your children are here!*
> *People of the market clear the way*
> *My lord is coming.*
> *My husband, I have arrived.*
> *Laroye, I have arrived*
> *Baraye, Baraye, Baraye!*

She wailed with a shrillness that shook the earth. The Oba's move was swift. In an instance of hesitation, capitulation or both — the Alayeru held the Eesa's left foot in a scissors

66

embrace, and the eminent chief was floored. The crowd roared as the Eesa sprang to his feet. He ran to the Balogun or generalismo of Aiyeru's army asking for justice: 'The corn cob floored me,' he cried. 'The corn-cob did it for the kabiyesi,' the women from the Eesa's compound — who had thrown a handful of corn-cobs on the floor — sang. The crowd laughed them to scorn as tradition demanded. The first dramatic irony of the day had merely been enacted, and others were set to follow.

The party of revellers arrived in our compound just before dusk. The big-parlour like the entire compound had received several transformations. Pity — I thought bitterly — if only the poor denizens of Origi's compound knew the people they were trying to impress. The scrubbings to the walls still left them shabby, and it's hard to imagine if they did any good. Ceremonial straw mats were spread everywhere, and people sat in groups of tens and twenties eating and drinking. On both halves of the sprawling veranda were the easy chairs and the three-seater sofa from the big-parlour. Already installed in the easy chairs were the head of Origi compound and other dignitaries from our compound. The sofa — which was decorated with the best of Maami-Agba's *aso-oke* — was reserved for my mother and father. Maami-Agba was seated in the easy chair to the left of the sofa, while Baami sat on the one to the right. Baami's senior aunt and my father's younger sister sat next to Maami-Agba in order of their seniority. If Maami-kekere's face was a mask of concentration earlier on, Maami-Agba's demeanour was one of contrite spirituality. Her calmness bespoke an inner turmoil that only the discerning eye could unmask. In his speech earlier in the day the Alayeru had spoken of the arrival of the town on the world stage. But in Maami-Agba's countenance there was a different kind of satisfaction. Like the proverbial *alágemo* — she appears to be saying — albeit without words — that she has helped in interpreting the world — our world — but the real task is to change it! That task she was willing to bequeath to those of her children that remained at home and the one she has slaved so much — in physical and spiritual terms — to see to this day.

67

Like Simeon waiting for the Consolation of Israel — she appears to be saying to her God at last:

> Lord, now You are letting your
> servant depart in peace,
> According to Your word;
> For my eyes have seen Your salvation!

The few remaining *Alágbède* of my grandfather's generation were present in a special way. They had disagreed with Baami — I later learnt — about honouring and holding a sacrifice to Ogun — the patron god of their vocation in our compound. But at Maami-Agba's intervention Baami was forced to give up:

'I don't know what your father would have said to them if he were here,' Maami-Agba was said to have told her son. 'His spirit watched over your brother in lands that you and I have never, and may never see. They mean well in wanting to honour his memory, so we must let them.'

The neck of the dog that was consequently severed appeared so huge that some in the crowd had placed bets that the old priest wouldn't achieve the severance in one stroke. 'That would be taboo,' one neighbour said to another.

'But the Church!' Baami was said to have cried: 'You are...'

'I'm the leader of the women, and you're the Church Secretary — so what? The pastor — if he has anything to say concerning this — would speak to me first before coming to you. So why are you worried,' Maami-Agba surmised, and silenced her son.

Now the stage is set and the oldest *Àgbède* in Aiyeru held the glittering machete that must sever the head of the prized dog from its body in one swoop as tradition demands. Failure to achieve the clean swoop was taboo and ill-omen. The man staggered, blinked hard and achieved divine sublimity just as the dog was stretched to its elastic limit for him to strike. The aim was perfect and without prevarication. The acolyte that held the dog's upper body staggered and fell as the crowd roared 'Ògún yè!' The party began in earnest as *bata* drums heralded and proclaimed the deity's triumphant entry into

68

Origi's compound. The old priest enacted a gig which the crowd applauded, thus signalling the commencement of another round of festivity.

'But putting aside all prevarications — we're at our best when we subsume none of our social or cultural heritage!' Mama Sarafa said to her neighbour.

'By which you mean that we mustn't be rooted in any particular view of the world — I suppose?' the neighbour responded miffed.

'Depends on what you mean by rootedness,' Mama Sarafa replied.

'Stop playing with words my friend!' the neighbour screamed: 'Do you want to call this abomination in a Christian household culture or irreligiousity? The oldest woman in that house should be ashamed of herself for allowing this abomination to take place.'

'I call it history my friend. It's a piece of family history that has just been reenacted here. If you want to know where you are, you must know where you are coming from — otherwise you would never know where you're going!' Mama Sarafa rounded.

It was past midnight before the last sets of revellers trickled out of our compound. The family sat together at last in the big-parlour, and my mind raced back to Aiyeru of the immediate past when memories of my parents was nothing more than a memory. Once she overcame her phobia — even Liz began to enjoy the atmosphere of our father's upbringing. She now slept in Maami-Agba's aged arms as if she'd found an eternal home. If I wasn't Olatunji and the six year old that she held her arms wasn't seven and a half years my junior even I could have sworn that the child in her arms was Motunde. My eyes locked into Maami-Agba's in warm embrace. She appeared to be reading my mind and smiled. Ralph's head rested between our father's younger sister's legs as he was also beginning to dose off. Liz whimpered and my mother moved to relieve Maami-Agba of her burden. The matriach waved her off, and cleared her aged throat. The look of satisfaction on Baami's face was tinged with the slightest hint of irony — albeit a self-reflexive one.

When she spoke eventually, Maami-agba's 'go into the world and preach the gospel' speech resembled an inaugural. But you could also call it a benediction. But whether as benediction or inaugural she appeared to be saying that she has reached the end of her tether. The balance the family struck this day — between tradition, history and religion — she said — should be preserved. She invoked the spirit of the dead *Àgbède* per excellence — the progenitor — whom she said might not be with us tonight — physically that is — but in spirit. She was hardly perturbed by the Judas look on my father's face nor the Thomas one which Baami wore. This is her annunciation and she has conquered death — she appears to be saying — before annunciating her gospel. He who believes shall be saved and the doubters would be damned! Our senior aunt sat resolute — equally proud — and you could be forgiven if you thought of her as the Daniel who purposed in his heart that he would neither defile himself with the portion of the king's delicacies, nor with the wine that he alone drank! My mother, Maami-kekere and our junior aunt on the other hand resembled a triumvirate — a triumvirate of Hananiah or Shadrach, Mishael or Meshach and Azariah or Abed-nego! 'Let us lay aside every weight, and the sin which so easily ensnares us, and let us run with endurance the race that is set before us' — appears to be the critical and creative manifesto of this triumvirate! Enduring the cross, despising the shame until they're sitted on top of the tyrants in their lives would play a prominent role in the campaign of the triumvirate. At last, Maami-agba prayed in a voice I scarcely recognised to be hers and in a way that I've never heard her pray before. As she named every member of the family either here or long gone, she implored her God and the spirit of her ancestors to be with them all.

It was hardly possible to have her to myself and vice-versa — before the journey back to Port-city. But when we did, she went straight to the point as I expected she would: 'How is life with your parents?' she asked breathlessly.

'I don't know Maami — I really don't know,' I replied equally breathless.

'How could you?' she said as if to sympathise with my fears, but added: 'The world is changing, and even I find it difficult to recognise the son that I sent out ten years ago. But you must always remember that I raised you right — remember Motunde, and remember me too — for I would soon be gone. You must run with endurance the race that is set before you!'

'I will Maami — I certainly will,' I replied without knowing what I was saying.

Five

Michael the destroyer flew across the living-room, and the hell he'd reduced the garden to was instantly transferred into the house. Just how so little a being could cause such pandemonium has always been a marvel. His diminutive two and a half feet frame appears to be made of solid bones and no flesh. The day the relentless five year old nearly knocked the life out of Bukola's grandmother — the great Ekiti witch of Bukola's mother's distaste — who made the mistake of her life trying, rather affectionately, to catch Michael while in full speed remains one of the memorable days in the family's contemporary history.

The age laden Ekiti-witch tumbled, mercifully enough, on the three-seater settee, did a somersault before landing in a state far too scary for a woman of her age. Houseboy Christopher discovered Bukola's grandmother in her prostrate state minutes later, groaning in severe pain. Bukola's chartered accountant father heard his mother's groan from the first of the five bedroom duplex and ran as fast as his legs would carry him downstairs.

'What is the matter, Mama?' he asked his mother.

'Your boy Bamidele! Your boy — that boy of yours...,' the woman groaned.

'I thinks she means Michael Sir,' Christopher said.

'Yes, yes, yes! What did Michael do?' Bukola's father asked impatiently.

'He fell me. I was only trying to stop him...'

'Maami, how many times have I told you not to attempt catching Michael when he's in flight. Neither the mother nor I who are much younger than you do that but you just wouldn't listen. Okay, just lie still and let me get the first aid box.'

'Here. Touch here Bamidele — I think my bone is broken here,' Bukola's grandmother said, pulling her son's fingers to examine where the pain hurt the most.

72

'I see,' Bukola's father said: 'I'll fetch the box all the same. I hope we don't have to take you to Malosa orthopeadic hospital anyway. I don't even know if Lanre is on duty today.'

Bukola's grandmother spent seven days at Malosa, returning with two crutches and a heavily bandaged arm.

The party tonight promise to be a grand affair. You could see by the look on her face that Bukola's mother wasn't looking forward to the party. But Bukola's father returned from work brimming with enthusiasm. Cartons of beer were unloaded from his Peugeot 404 saloon car by his driver, Buroda Lekan and houseboy Christopher. Putting down his suitcase, Bukola's father went straight to his wife who was still surrounded by the pile of books from which she's been churning out a series of quotable quotes.

'I can see you've been working hard sweetheart. How's the thesis coming up,' he said bending down to kiss his wife.

'And howdy Omo-Ekiti and the Alayeru himself?' he said to Bukola and I.

'Welcome Sir,' we chorused, Bukola kneeling and I prostrating.

'You guys are hell bent on remaining rooted to this primitive affair,' Bukola's father said to no one in particular.

'I think it's a marked show of respect and besides it's our culture,' Bukola's mother said in defence of the age-old practice.

'Please darling, I'm looking forward to an evening of relaxation and not one of arguments and hypotheses. If you prefer to hang on to all those medieval stuff while the rest of the world is making giant strides, then that's your problem entirely. It's a democractic age though and I think I'm entitled to my opinions.'

'Just listen to that! Look here Dele, if you try to unpack all you've just said it wouldn't sound so democractic you know? It's just another ugly absolutism complete in it's culturally packaged ugly imperialism,' Bukola's mother's said looking livid.

'Oh No! — not tonight please. What have I said really to

73

warrant all that. What have you guys really been up to today?'

'Just a lot of medieval stuff that wouldn't be of interest to a cultured man-of-the-moment like you I suppose. But could you please mind your language in this house?'

It was a moonlit night — the full moon. The weather looked promising and the gentle breeze from the beach made Elizabethan Island the perfect place to be on a night like this. A pool of servants or houseboys as they're called, from the neighbouring houses including ours, laboured in white overalls and ridiculously tall hats laying rows of tables with shinning white clothes in a long neat line on the garden lawns. The tables laid, assortment of foods and drinks were placed on them in a very orderly manner. Soft Ebenezer Obey music castigating the rich of this earth who have refused to yield to the life of maximum enjoyment floated in the twilight air: 'Be certain, be assured that we found everything on earth and on this earth we shall abandon all, Chief Commander Obey reminded all listeners.

Cars began to arrive and Bukola's father who had since changed from the suited man of the office to an evening Mala-style-kaftan ready to play the perfect host resembled the quintessential Elizabethan Island socialite. Bukola's mother held her head in her hands still sitting on the carpeted floor where she had her last argument with Bukola's father.

'Darling the guests are arriving, and you really must change into something decent,' Bukola's father said. A look at his wife convinced him that he had not succeeded in communicating anything and he said as a follow up: 'Okay, okay, I'm sorry for upsetting you sweety — or do you want me to prostrate?'

'Yes, that would really help. At least it would show that you're beginning to learn some manners. Look Dele, I'm really not sure if I'm up to this thing tonight...it's becoming rather tedious and monotonous you know?...I mean...'

Before Bukola's mother could complete her statement my mother and father entered through the wide open flush doors — with Ralph and Liz trailing behind them like discarded placentas. Liz screamed at the top of her voice, nearly knocking our parents down, upon encountering Michael the destroyer who at that moment was descending the flight of stairs from the bedrooms. Michael ran back upstairs also screaming as if the whole thing had been prearranged causing Liz to give chase. Ralph who is two and three years respectively older than the pair looked apologetic, took in the scene and went after Liz and Michael.

'Ralph, be a good boy, and restrict those two to Mike's room for me — would you?' Bukola's mother asked.

'I'll try Auntie — I'll try,' Ralph replied without conviction. Upstairs the pandemonium had already begun.

'I've got a tom-boy for a daughter and this one here clearly should have been a girl,' my mother said pointing at me. 'And Tunji, by the way, I don't remember seeing you around the house at all today — where have you been?' she asked.

'Welcome Ma and Sir,' Bukola knelt while I prostrated. The two adults guffawed but Bukola's father was alarmed. The argument he'd had with Bukola's mother earlier was clearly at the back of his mind, a repeat performance of which he knew would definitely ruin his night.

'Bayo,' he said quickly changing the subject, 'how was the office today?'

'Well, what can one say — I guess we're managing,' my father replied — his mind obviously crowded with several thoughts threatening to pop out all at the same time.

'That makes you a manager — doesn't it?' Bukola's father said roaring at his own joke. 'By the way,' he went on, 'are all those Landrovers coming in for your office entirely meant for the National Planning Council or would some be given to other departments?' he asked.

'What do you mean? They're not even sufficient and we're expecting a consignment of another thirty-five next week. You know what Baluban roads are like — don't you? Majority of them would be ruined by the bad roads within a couple of months,' my father remarked.

'And bad driving,' Bukola's mother chorused.

'That's unfortunately true,' my father agreed.

'And six months later all would be auctioned to top

functionaries who by some miracle would be able to drive them for the next ten years,' Bukola's mother said.

Silence. Embarrassing silence. Since no one spoke, Bukola's mother went on to say. 'If we're really interested in a cure why don't we fix the roads first. Finish building a network of not-necessarily perfect but motorable roads before we start importing motor-vehicles? Or when would we stop putting the cart before the horse in every aspect of our national life?' she rounded. Before my father could reply, Bukola's father interjected suggesting it's time to take orders for drinks.

'Gulu!' my father said using his affectionate acronym for Gulder larger beer.

'Same for me,' Bukola's father said, before asking 'and the ladies?'

'White sparkling wine please,' my mother said smacking her lips as if the wine had already arrived.

'And should I get you the nativity drug darling?' Bukola's father asked his wife.

Bukola's mother said: 'Yes please — it contains none of the chemicals you all are about to swallow, so feel free to snigger as much as you can. Please serve me from the jug Joe the tapper brought yesterday. It's in the fridge.'

'Right O! Your obedient servant: Two same, one sparkling, and one not-so-sparkling,' Bukola's father recounted like a happy ten-year-old sent on a delightful errand. 'Tunji and Bukola — please help yourselves to some Coca-Cola or Fanta. Or would you rather tag-along with the native panacea — Gbogbònse!' Bukola's father said, walking away before anyone could answer.

'It was the serpent that stung humankind and turned us into victims of death,' the Chief Commander Ebenezer Obey wailed over the gramophone.

'You know the beauty of those lines for me is it's genderless rendition. I mean, it makes more sense than all that Adam and Eve jive,' Bukola's mother said to my mother.

'But that's a distortion of the Bible,' my mother replied.

'Why is it a distortion and not a correction?' Bukola's

mother fired back.

'Oh come-on Bunmi, don't start all that feminist nonsense again. I mean how would you begin to correct the Bible. You either accept it or you don't.'

'But Ebenezer Obey is a Christian....'

'Who has commited the heretical sin of distortion of the holy writ,' my mother corrected.

Out of sheer coincidence, the issue under discussion coincided with the advent of Dr. and Mrs. Fapeyi, well known members of the Adventist Movement. Dr. Lanre Fapeyi of Malosa orthopaedic hospital is widely believed to be the best orthopeadic surgeon in the whole of Baluba. But next to ordering or re-ordering dislocated or disordered muscles and joints, his only other passion is that of the Adventist credo. A teetotaller of the strictest discpline, Dr. Fapeyi and his equally sober wife are blessed with three sons who are carbon-copies of their mother and a daughter who looks like the father's Siamese-twin; a game which Dr. Fapeyi, despite his scientific credentials has dubbed unequal at best, and overtly unfair whenever he's piqued — which mercifully enough isn't often. The Fapeyi children are also a study in contrast when it comes to comparing them with the children of their fellow returnee friends and associates. The moment they settled down — the woman drinking Coca-Cola along with her daughter and one son while the other two sons opted for the frizzy Sprite and the father cuddled a glass of water — with the same affection with which he said 'H_2O' please, when Bukola's father took their orders. Mrs. Fapeyi entered the debate between my mother and Bukola's mother on the religious topic immediately they settled down:

'Well, I'm not saying that Ebenezer Obey is right or wrong,' Mrs. Fapeyi stated. 'But let's assume it's a distortion as you said, what about all the other distortions built into the body of Christian beliefs within the western framework — I mean things like Christmas, Easter, et cetera. Are they the only ones who can bend or distort the facts of Faith to suit their own socio-cultural framework?'

But the beginning of the party proper also meant the end of adults and kiddies interaction for the night. The children, it would seem, have been brought so that they can impress both their parents and their parents' friends as well as one another with how much they've advanced in their nursery and primary schools. First, they're fed, and allowed to drink to their satisfaction, and just before the various drivers begin to whisk the children back home to the waiting arms of house maids who would ensure that they're carefully tucked in bed, they're given the chance to perform or say goodnight to their parents and parents' friends in their own ways. The nursery groups always came first, reciting one nursery rhyme after the other until the audience of standing parents clap and clap them off the stage:

Bla bla black sheep
Have you any wool?
Yes sir, yes sir three bags full!
One for the master, one for the...! *et cetera*

Twinkle, twinkle little star
How I wonder what you are....

were endlessly sung.

'You know, you really can't appreciate how romantic that nursery rhyme sounds until you hear it recited under the Baluban sky on a moonlit night like this and you can actually see the stars twinkling and sparkling in the sky,' one extraordinarily impressed father said.

'No you can't,' the other replied.

'I'm so glad we're back.'

The Fapeyi children sang an Adventist hymn and received a mild applause. Bukola's mother beckoned at Bukola and I to go forward and deliver our over-rehearsed coup de grace entitled, 'In groups of threes so are friends!'

Meta meta lore o! — I lead
Eeeeh! — Bukola chorused
One invited me to sleep on the bare floor
Eeeeeeh!

The other beckoned me to the communal mat
Eeeeeeeh!
Yet another offered me the chest
Eeeeeh!
With my utterly frolicked eyes I pitched my tent with the
chestful one!
Eeeeeeeeeeeeeeeeeeh!
Meta meta lore O!
I've encountered the sea, I've seen numerous beaches!
etc., etc.

The applause was wild, and Bukola courtesied while I bowed.

I made it to Bukola's house everyday at the crack of dawn. The days my mother stopped me using one feeble excuse or the other were inexorably christened days of misery.

'Why don't you see it as an exchange programme,' I said one day.

'Meaning what?'she asked, her eyes blazing.

'Well, since Michael the destroyer is almost always here, and I love being there that's the...!'

'Wrong on all counts,' she said before I could finish. 'And I don't want to hear you call that boy the destroyer again — is that okay? He's just full of life and that's a lot more than one can say about all you Baluba brought up kids and your love for the mediaeval stuff you call culture.'

I was going to say concerning the destroyer that I didn't invent the name, but thought otherwise. Instead I said: 'Destructive energy is easy to praise from the bestial human viewpoint. It's in everyman but some of us have simply been taught to suppress that aspect of our human nature. It's not cowardice.'

'Oh! And are you a man now? And have we reached the point where you must answer to whatever I say word for word, and point by point?'

Pity, I said to myself. I possess none of Bukola's dexterity — the sort of tenacious inner strength with which she broke her own mother.

I'm engaged in too many balancing acts, I thought bitterly. Whenever I'm all out for Liz her frame changes mysteriously to Motunde's, and whenever this woman starts posing accusing questions at me, Maami-Agba's admonitions about letting her down would start reverberating in my head.

'I'm terribly sorry if I've offended you,' I said prostrating. In response my mother chuckled seemingly chuffed.

'See? Who told you to apologise now? That's what you call the quiet resolution of your upbringing — I sup-pose? An inability to sustain anything — whether in the form of attack or defense. A prostrate culture — always apologising!'

The bile in my mouth turned to guile. The kitchen floor trembled and tumbled. When I looked up it was Maami-Agba standing there telling me about Babalola's crusade and her suffering *inter alia* — the entire story about healing without medicine. The *lùkúlùkú* epidemic, and how our gods failed when they — she and others — needed them most. Bukola's mother's theory sprang up from within me and an inner bell warned me to remain sceptical —

'Rationalisation or theory'? I asked.

'What is the difference?' the voice asked in return.

'The former is an excuse, the latter a possibility,' I replied.

'Then take what you need — when it's necessary to rationalize don't wait, and the moment it becomes necessary for you to theorize — match on. But remember that there's no theory without practice, and there's no such thing as a cultural practice that doesn't possess it's own synchronic as well as diachronic theoretical focus even if the practitioners are unable or unwilling to articulate those theoretical premises,' the voice rounded. My mother's voice brought me sharply back to body terrestrial.

'I don't know why you stand there gazing at the floor like Mama Olu's goat. I said more than five minutes ago that you can leave for your second home, or isn't that what you wanted to hear?' she asked.

I laughed as if she'd cracked the funniest joke ever. Her shock registered as she said: 'And what's so funny — Native Son?'

'What you just said,' I replied still smiling.

'Which is?' she quizzed.

'Looking at the floor like Mama Olu's goat,' I replied.

'Oh, I see. The problem with you natives is that you really think that because one has been away for so long, we're never able to participate in your cultural orgy or sayings anymore — that we've turned our back on our culture entirely. You're dead wrong there. I know far more about Aiyeru or Baluban culture than you can ever pick up or understand.'

'I'm glad to hear that Maami. But which aspect of it do you think we need most to survive this modern dispensation,' I said, hating my own condescending tone.

'Change that tongue of yours to begin with. I wonder why it's so difficult for you to say Mummy like all civilized children do. And don't talk to me in that condescending tone — okay?'

It's no use, I sighed. It's never any use. I was halfway through the living-room when I heard her voice saying: 'Tell Bunmi — I mean Bukola's mum to lend us that Lamidi Baba Sala record again — Tunji. And don't let me send for you before you come back.'

'Which of the Baba Sala records,' I shouted back.

'*Orun Mo ru!*' she screamed.

Well, that summarizes it — doesn't it? I thought bitterly again. Native humour, native food, but never any attempt to domesticate other aspects of entity. Wholesale abandonment in one realm — selective accommodation in another — that's the returnee's cultural practice. The voice is right, there must be a theory behind it, even if the practitioners are unable or unwilling to articulate these theoretical premises. Neither here nor there — even within the same genre the imbalance remains mind boggling: Baba Sala and not Ogunmola; Ade Love but not Duro Ladipo; Ranko baby preferred to Hubert Ogunde, and the shutters or boundaries if you like remain forever rigid and ill-defined. One is heresy — an integral aspect of our better forgotten past — the other a mere contri- bution to the 'tribal rock, of poverty, of rite' — permissible relics from our storehouse of culture as long as they can be transformed into commercial objects for the entertainment industry!

At Bukola's I met mother and daughter seated, laughing like

two bosom sisters in contrite mischief.

'Good morning Ma,' I said prostrating.

'The son of Aiyeru himself. How are you this morning — Àlàbí òlá,' Bukola said instead of the mother who continued to smile.

'So because of the two months that separates us in age, you think I should prostrate to you — Bukola are you sick?' I asked jokingly.

'Why not! Those are sixty-two solid days you know. And how many hours do you think that might amount to? You'll need the combine sense of all of Aiyeru's mathematicians, QED, *et al.,* to calculate what we're talking about in minutes — barring the seconds.'

'Rigged. The whole thing is rigged. You were born on the 29th day of February — the year of independence — a day which occurs only once every four years, and I arrived on 22nd April — so where did you get this sixty-two days fallacy from?' I asked.

Bukola cried: 'Where were you the whole of March? And April was nearly, I mean literally over before you stumbled out — so don't tell me about fallacious calculations. An *asiwaju* is an *asiwaju,* and you better start respecting your elders — full stop! It's the only commandment without a promise or something like that.'

'Wrong again,' I said. 'Between Taiwo and Kehinde would you care to tell me who happens to be the oldest?'

'Sit down Tunji,' Bukola's mother said: 'or are you going to carry on the entire bantering of today on your feet?'

'No Ma, and thank you. But this girl is infuriating,' I said feigning severe anger.

'Listen to that Maami. Who is this girl? I'm his senior sister for goodness sake — I drank the waters of this world before him.' Bukola reiterated.

'How is your mother Tunji?' Bukola's mother said trying to change the subject.

'She's fine Ma, and she sends her greetings to you and the family. She also said that I should bring the Baba Sala record with me on my way home.'

'You see that now. So you had such an important and sacred

82

message to deliver and you just stood there sickeningly rude to your elders.'

'Enough of that Bukola. Tunji won the argument fair and square, if you ask for my opinions without taking sides. First, as he said, your figures are rigged, and the analogy he posed about Taiwo and Kehinde is sound and valid to me, but you evaded that completely.' Bukola's mother said.

'I didn't evade anything. Okay leave my figures out of it and let us concentrate on the Taiwo and Kehinde analogue as you said. To begin with, I'm not this boy's Taiwo, and he's not my Kehinde, so the analogy doesn't hold — full stop!' Bukola countered.

'And who is this boy? Look, the day this mouth of yours is going to put you in police custody, you'll see. Before I come to bail you or allow anyone to do so, I will make sure that you're allowed to suffer.'

Like the transformation sweeping the Baluban nation — Bukola and I — within the six or seven years since the returnees' return — have had our fair share of transformations. Families have been ripped apart and communal ties destroyed. The age it appears had an unending chain of transformation of lives whether in the epistemological or signifying realms. Majority of the returnees remained rooted in their fanatically held belief, that bits and pieces of what we called Baluban culture belonged to the mediaeval past. Bukola blossomed into a handsome lady — combining her father's regal height with the mother's intellect and philosophical dispensation. In our final year at King's school and Queen's College respectively, we both sought more and more clarifications from Bukola's mother on a plethora range of subjects. As Bukola's mother's distaste for Elizabethan Island and all that it held grew, so did our own appetite for her centrifugal socio-cultural psyche that would rescue our own from further heresies. The mythological pantheon of the colonial past and the unending antics of our neocolonial present left each of us — including Bukola's mother — extremely flustered to say the least. Nothing has changed you might say since the days Chiefs used to sell their own people and were celestially happy with the proceeds of their dastardly trade!

83

'It's no use with you two,' Bukola's mother said finally: 'But Tunji, how many times is your mother going to listen to the Baba Sala record? I thought I'd persuaded her to hear Duro Ladipo's *Oba Ko So*? I'm not taking anything away from Alawada, but the Sango story is poetry of the highest order.'

'With due respect Ma, you may have to go tell that one on the mountain — especially where my mother is concerned. The mildest of Ladipo's shows doesn't interest her at all — not even Hugo von Hofmannsthal's German version of *Everyman* adapted for the Ladipo company by Obotunde Ijimere.'

'I'm sure you kids understand by now that the whole thing is a very complex and at times even complicated matter. The selective nature of these anti-Baluban posturings has to do with our self-hatred. As perceptive and deeply spiritual as Dr. Lanre Fapeyi happens to be when I told him about Pierre Fatumbi's seminal publication, *Awon Ewe Osanyin: Yoruba Medicinal Leaves*, he simply dismissed the whole thing as esoteric nonsense. *Dílógún: Brazilian Tales of Yoruba Divination Discovered in Bahia* by the same author staggered him a bit, and I can understand why. You see, the paradox of it all is that not a single one of us — so called returnees — can claim not to have suffered severely from deep-seated racism in the land of our sojourn. And yet, we're the lucky ones — because we've been able to return. I tell you, there are thousands left out there who may never make it back — not out of choice but out of compulsion.' Bukola's mother explained.

'What do you mean by that Ma? Why would anyone be unable to return out of compulsion — I don't understand?' I said.

'Well Tunji, that's the nature of our own Middle-Passage. Deep-seated issue but not impossible to understand or explain. The Middle-Passage is a metaphor — a metaphor for dispossession, and in physical terms it represents the entire vessel used to transport you from the point of origin to the land of your ultimate dispossession. But the passage is also a gulf that you must recross in order to recoup or reappropriate what was lost. But, the process of reappropriation is fraught with practical and theoretical impediments. At best, you can compare it to the act of scooping a broken egg from the floor really. Many would try — but the majority stupefied and transfixed by the enormity of what is involved in the process wouldn't even dare raise a finger — and that's the way the creators of this culpable world would rather have it; no step forward, but several steps backwards every waking day.'

'Maami, please tell Tunji the story of 'I would rather die' — please! Tunji, you'll love this. It's about a woman — an old woman that Maami tried to help onto a bus,' Bukola said with sparkling, mischievious eyes.

"So what happened?' I asked.

'Yes, Bukola you're right,' the mother agreed with her daughter that the story is particularly relevant to the issue under discussion. 'It's a classic tale of how you're gradually abused and reduced to a bestial level and you develop without knowing it your own version of what a friend of mine has termed anti-racist racism in a depressing, rather inhuman way. The story must have occurred during the second year of our sojourn, and the winter that year was rather severe. There was snow everywhere, and the weather several degrees below zero degree freezing point for several weeks. I got out that fateful morning and walked briskly to the nearest bus stop. I got on the bus within minutes, but being the rush hour, the bus was packed full, and I couldn't find a seat. I stood close to the entrance of the bus clinging to one of the rear railings with one hand and clutching my heavy bag with the other. At the next stop people got down, and others waited to get on board. And there she was — the old white lady, trembling in the cold, obviously intent on getting onto the crowded bus. I looked at her, and I was overcome with emotion. I thought of my mother — my grandmother in fact — and respectfully extended a hand — a human hand! — to help lift her onto the bus. She looked up, saw my smiling face and shrank back instantly: 'No! No! No! I'll rather die! she screamed in such a lively high-pitched voice, I thought couldn't still inhabit such a withered body. I froze several degrees beneath the freezing weather and felt a trickle in my panties as all eyes both from the bottom and top decks of the crowded bus focused on the ensuing drama. The white bus conductor manoeuvred his way

85

from the front of the bottom deck where he'd been collecting fares. He stood behind me and gave the old lady his bare hands which she preferred to my gloved black hands. 'Thank you darling, the old lady pouted as if the conductor was her own son and climbed onto the bus.' Bukola's mother narrated, her eyes sad, her countenance heavy.

'So what did the other passengers say?' I said really incensed.

'It's none of their business — my help was unsolicited and the insult I received thoroughly well deserved. It's a process as I said, gradual but devastating and that's merely one among numerous examples. That's why I remain sceptical about these cannibalistic-liberal-humanist-lot propounding this anti-racist racism theory. It's simply a slippery slope and I would be extremely wary to travel down that road: 'when even a goat or a sheep looks back, as our people say, 'it's got to send torrents of curses to whoever deserves them,' Bukola's mother rounded.

'Well, Tunji — that's not the end of the story — and Maami, I want you to complete the story first,' Bukola said.

'The bus moved on. The old lady stood right behind me. Very soon, seats — or shall I say — a seat became vacant in front of me. Naturally, I would have offered it to the old lady, but not after what had just happened. I sat down pulling my heavy bag onto my lap and instinctively drawing my legs together. My high-heeled shoe stretched back and the heels, without my knowledge, rested on the old lady's foot. I heard groaning sounds, but didn't dare look back. At last the bus stopped and I'd reached my destination. I rose and my entire weight travelled down to my heels one of which still held the old lady's foot in painful embrace. 'Hoof! Hoof! I heard, and didn't realise the damage I'd caused until I was on my way out of the bus. The lady turned yellow, then greyish pale. As she bent to massage her aching foot our eyes met, and locked in an instance of the most painful embrace, as if both pairs of eyes were saying simultaneously 'Hell-O and Good-bile at the same time.'

'Rather die! Yes rather die!' Bukola shouted, as if the events were just unfolding, and she a living witness.

'But Dr. Lanre Fapeyi's experience was rather more lurid and sickening,' Bukola's mother announced.

'What happened? What happened to Dr. Fapeyi?' I asked my hair standing on tenterhooks.

'Well, Lanre as you know is one of the best orthopaedic surgeons in the world, as far as Western science and technology is concerned. He has always been deeply spiritual as you both happen to know.'

'And Tunji, do you know that Dr. Fapeyi was one of Maami's very first suitors, and Baami even knows about it?' Bukola said mischievously.

'Mind your own blasted business — *Omo Esu lasanlasan!* Anyway Tunji are you listening to me — because I'm not interested in the same thing that this child of mischief is talking about?' Bukola's mother complained.

'Yes, yes, I agree. But we may have to revisit that other angle later. It's quite intriguing,' I said.

'You're certainly not revisiting any angle that's none of your business,' Bukola's mother said firmly. 'And you better listen to me now you two idlers — sacrilegious busy-bodies!'

'Oh No!' Bukola and I screamed as if the whole thing was prearranged.

'I wouldn't mind being called all that if that will get us to the bottom of this other tale. I mean Maami wasn't it true that you both were quite a flame, and you just dropped him like that? Really, you're *Obinrin Odale,* and the story should be handed over to Kola Ogunmola's company — it's a tragic tale, and it can only be handled well by a company of that magnitude. You're like the mouse who was in a sworn pact with *Ifá* and betrayed *Ifá* — you shouldn't go scot free!' Bukola rambled on.

Smiling, Bukola's mother said: 'Well, you certainly know how to get carried away — don't you? The controversy you're stirring is dead and buried and all the *dramatis personae* happy and glad to have it buried. So what is your problem — the sympathiser wailing more than the bereaved?'

'Yes! Yes, we're certainly in the era of name-calling — *abi* Tunji? But call me what you like, but I and my sister and brother deserve to know why we have an accountant for a father and not one of the world's most brilliant orthopaedic surgeons!'

'Hey! See me, see this ranting clown O! Have you ever heard the prayer — the matter that we know neither the leg nor the hand of, may the murky part of it never become ours to undo?' Bukola's mother asked.

'But as I hope to have convinced you eminent members of the jury, I'm clearly an interested party in this matter. The charge, my Lord, is infanticide, and the details involve why a group of deserving kids have ended up with one set of genes causing them to be depressed and argumentative on the one hand, and another set inducing gross retardation in them on the other, are now seeking well deserved redress from the source(s) of their retardation and abuse. The prosecution, my Lord, will like to begin by asking your grace to subpoena Dr. (Mrs.) Osanyinbunmi Okediran, nee Osanyin to state all she knows about this matter,' Bukola stated, treating me as both judge and jury.

'My Lord,' Bukola's mother said, determined to invalidate Bukola in her own game: 'this preposterous charge is ridiculous. The prosecution is neither focused nor articulate. The charge amounts to asking why Okediran is your father and not Fapeyi, and who ever heard of such a question. The prosecution, my Lord, is clearly suffering from what amounts to a delusion of grandeur, besides being...'

'Objection sustained. Case suspended till further notice,' I said mockingly.

'And my Lord, the defendant would also like the prosecution to withdraw forthwith and desist from further reference to the defendant as Doctor. The defendant is a doctoral candidate still working on her thesis, and has never stated before the prosecution or anyone else that she has been awarded the degree.'

'Sustained. Would the prosecution state before the open court that the appellation of doctor is hereby withdrawn?' I added.

'You're the worst judge I've ever seen. You will ruin even the most perfect case anyone might have,' Bukola said.

'You're just a bad loser,' Bukola's mother replied smiling. 'Well, having lost the case in an open court, and only marginally escaped being libellous, you should just count yourself lucky, and cease from further harrassment of the defendant as the eminent jurist has said.'

'We shall see. She who fights and runs away will definitely live to fight another day,' Bukola surmised.

'As I was saying before that very rude interruption, besides being one of the best surgeons, Dr. Lanre Fapeyi would also qualify as one of the very first blackman to ever attempt putting mangled white bones together,' Bukola's mother said ignoring Bukola's pained demeanour.

'Lanre knew his job, and not even his worst detractors would deny that. The hospital where he worked was prepared to keep him forever if it were possible. Ask him how life is treating him or how he's treating the whole point of existence, and his famous reply never changing, never faltering would be 'disorder must be ordered. Day in day out, Lanre would purr over X-rays producing simple solutions to complicated disorderliness in every muscle, every joint of the human body when he wasn't actually in the theatre practically patching these joints. Lanre sat in his office day and night and long after his colleagues had left for their homes to the warm embrace of family life. He sat there theorising and practicing at the same time. Case file upon case files landed on Lanre's desk, and his rate of success each time was phenomenal. Lanre's wife, bored stiff at home, but an epitome of patience like her husband bore his absence gracefully, but took recourse to child rearing. 'How's the old incubator? — I used to tease him whenever we met.'

'I can see you two never stopped loving each other,' Bukola stated matter of factly.

'Mind your own rotten business,' I said trying to stop Bukola from distracting her mother any further. Instead Bukola screamed: 'A biased judge! The world is broken!' And we all laughed.

'Thank you Tunji,' Bukola's mother said and continued. 'Lanre naively — rather naively — assumed that the fact that he never met any of his patients face to face until they've been anaesthetized and placed on the operating table was both a sign of respect for the seriousness of his office and above all the sanctity of his role. That a whole scientific establishment made up of colleagues, junior doctors, student doctors, nurses and aides could conspire against a single human being staggered and at the same time threatened Lanre's sanity. But Lanre walked into the male ward in a very untypical fashion one afternoon, and revelations poured galore. He knew the patient he wanted, and he walked straight to his bedside to re-read his case history.'

'Who are you?' the patient asked.

'Putting on his best medical ethics, Lanre happily announced to the bewildered patient that he was Dr. Fapeyi who would be operating on him the following day. 'There must be a mistake here, the bewildered patient announced, and went on to say that he thought Dr. Gordon was in charge here. 'Yes, Lanre announced, 'Dr. Gordon is my assistant and he would be there to assist me tomorrow when we ... In obvious ignorance of the unravelling mystery, Lanre turned to the bewildered patient's neighbour, and asked how he was recovering from his own surgery of the day before.'

'I'm fine, really fine. That Dr. Gordon is a genius — a true miracle worker,' the neighbour explained.

'Yes, we work together,' Lanre repeated, 'and as I said John Gordon is my assistant.'

'You mean you were there when I was operated on?' the neighbour asked the increasingly bemused Lanre Fapeyi.

'I wasn't just there as a spectator,' Lanre said, beginning to feel slightly irritated: 'I led the team of surgeons, nurses and aides who took care of you. They all work under me,' Lanre explained. The neighbour's countenance dropped, and aware-ness — a painful awareness began to dawn on both the erudite surgeon and his patients.

'Do you have a problem with me operating on you?' Lanre finally asked after the minute or so of embarrassing silence.

'Problem? Did you say problem?' the now agitated neighbour charged: 'How dare you lay your ...your...those hands on me?'

'What hands?' Lanre asked, examining his hands as if he was seeing them for the first time.

'Yes, those hands. How dare you touch — how dare you...them...on me?' the neighbour wanted to know. A nurse passed by and Lanre called out to her.

'Laura, just a minute here if you don't mind,' Lanre said.

'Hell-O Doctor. How can I help you?' Nurse Laura asked.

'Oh dear! Oh dear!' the now livid neighbour gasped severally: 'what is this place turning into?' he asked no one in particular.

Nurse Laura caught the tail-end of the neighbour's spoken consternation and anger, and awareness dawned on her. She marched to John Gordon's office with Lanre following closely behind.

'John, what dastardly game have you all being playing in this rotten place for the past four years?' Lanre wanted to know.

'Hey Lanray, what could have upset you so much?' the genuinely shocked John Gordon who has never seen Lanre raise his voice in four years of treacherous partnership wanted to know what could have made the saintly surgeon so angry.

'Yes, the stuff fed to the patients is what has upset me so much Johnny, and I demand an immediate explanation from all concerned now!' Lanre explained, his eyes already misty.

Gordon's countenance dropped. He stood there, slouched midway between his chair and desk like a man transfixed by a bolt of lightening.

'Yes, may Sango strike you all dead!' Lanre cursed before storming out of Gordon's office. Gordon's voice trailed Lanre to his office where he'd begun to put his professional paraphernalia together. He heard Gordon saying: 'We meant it for the best of all. Believe me Lan-ray we respect you. We all do — we truly respect you. But the patients — we did it for the patient. You see, Lan-ray they would never understand!'

'One look at Tinuke told me that the heavens had fallen. The usually calm and collected Community Health Officer was to say the least a shadow of her real self.

'What is the matter Tinu?' I asked really alarmed. My heart flew into my mouth as I waited for the bombshell I was convinced Tinu was about to release — what would it be, I asked myself, while waiting for Tinu to calm down — Hiroshima? Nagasaki? Or just another protracted Vietnam debacle? Tinu sobbed silently but stoically,' Bukola's mother continued.

'It's Lanre — Oh! my God — Bunmi, it's Lanre! Lanre has killed me. I doubt if he's going to make it. They've finished him. Our world is shattered,' Tinu wailed.

'Now Tinu, don't over excite you — remember your condition and you really must calm down, I said trying to think. Every nerve, every vein on Tinu's fragile body stood still as she shivered in the autumn air mumbling, 'what shall I do now? Tell me Bunmi what shall I do?'

By some miracle, Tinuke survived and so did the baby in her. We walked to the nearest hospital where Tinuke was admitted at once. Her child was in dire stress, the doctor announced, and has to be brought out immediately: 'leave it to us,' the doctor smiled trying to encourage me. 'I will, I will certainly leave it to you,' I said severally.

Tinu was wheeled into the operating theatre and the matter was entirely out of my hands. I phoned Bamidele to tell him what had happened, and that I may not be home at all that night. A delicate affair, since the wound of the rivalry between him and Lanre hadn't quite healed. I had to be careful how I broke the news to Dele — making it clear that it was Tinu that came to me. When he heard that Lanre was at a psychiatric hospital in the East-end, he was touched and came to join me at the hospital where Tinu was being operated. By the time Lanre got to me, Tinu had been relieved of her seven month old burden: 'daughter and mother,' the doctor announced, 'are doing fine, and both at rest.' What an irony, I thought bitterly. Lanre who loves his three boys had always wanted a daughter. Dear Lord, please let Lanre live, I prayed like the child I was convinced I had become. Dele and I were allowed to see Tinuke for five minutes. Titilope lay in an incubator, a bewildering array of tubes and gadgets passed into many parts of her tiny body.

'Well, that's that,' Dele said: 'We can't hope for anything better than this out of the set up here. Let's go after their husband and father,' Dele said as he dragged me gently out of the intensive care unit.

The one or so hour trip from the West-end where Tinu and Titi laid, to the East where we knew next to nothing how Lanre was faring was without doubt one of the longest journeys of my entire life. The autumn air was cold but not bitting. Dele and I found nothing to say to each other. I was happy and glad — for once — to be treated the way Dele has always wanted and liked to treat me; my diminutive frame eclipsed by his giant stature. He'd taken his light jacket off and wrapped it around me, while holding me like a delicate goblet.

'So how did Lanre find out?' Dele said as we were approaching the last tube station where we'll get down and carry on to the East-End Psychiatric Hospital by bus.

'By accident I suppose. Tinu couldn't tell me much before she collapsed,' I said.

We walked out of the tube station and the bus we needed arrived just a few minutes after we got to the bus stop. Dele pushed me ahead, striding confidently behind me as I climbed to the upper deck of the half empty bus. I stood beside an empty seat to allow Dele in first so that he could sit by the window. Neither of us had been to a psychiatric hospital in this land, and we were filled with varying degrees of trepidation about what we might find. The main building was a tall, imposing structure of several floors. We went in through the main building, and stopped at the reception desk, where a calm ashen faced middle-age man was in charge.

'We're here to see a patient,' Dele announced.

'Name? Main ward or intensive care?' the nurse asked.

'I'm afraid we only have the name,' Dele said.

'Must be a fresh case then,' the nurse remarked. The word fresh stuck out of all he said, and I couldn't help but think of my wounds as a child.

'Yes, must have been brought here about this time yesterday. His name is Dr. Lanre Fapeyi,' Dele said slowly.

'African?' the man quizzed.

'Yes, Baluban!' Dele choroused.

'Then I know who you want. He's quite calm now, but you can't take chances — you know?' the man said as if trying to co-opt us into becoming accomplices in a fairly complex *fait accompli*. The effect wasn't lost on Dele who shook his head sadly.

Lanre sat in a straitjacket in a brightly lit windowless room. He sat on what you can describe more appropriately as an iron-colt rather than a bed. It was clear that he hadn't slept for a long time, and he lowered his eyes the moment we approached.

'Don't come too close — I'm quite dangerous,' Lanre said and I was relieved.

'Buroda,' Dele said in deference to the five or so years that separated him and Lanre in age as tradition demands: 'We're so sorry. We came as soon as we heard.'

'Thank you Dele. The ordeal reads like the Book of Job — doesn't it? I hope this people will give me a Bible instead of having me bound in this thing. I've finished with them. But I'm familiar enough with their *modus operandi* to know that you dare not proclaim that you're cured of your madness. It's like dousing a raging inferno with petrol — or have you ever seen the mouse win a case in a court presided over by the cat? From Freud to Foucault, not to say a word about the confused characters who run institutions like this, they're still pretending not to understand how closely intertwined madness is with their civilization. Don't you know the lynch-pin of orthodox liberalism? à la Blake:

> The man who makes his law a curse
> Will surely die by that law!

So onward civilization: no permanent friend, but we must nurse and nurture a few permanent enemies to keep alive the arms industry. Anything, everything can be sacrificed on the altar of socio-political, most particularly economic expediency. That's why they could conspire to exterminate my own family while I was busy putting their own mangled bodies together!

A history of insanity in the age of reason will show that even the speech given to madness is contemporaneous — both in time and structure — with that which they've announced to themselves that God is dead!'

I was more than relieved to hear him talk like that — the bitterness in his voice notwithstanding. It was only then that I knew that Lanre was merely being punished for a moment's outrage — even though I still didn't know the ways and manner in which he executed or expressed that outrage.

'How is Tinuke?' Lanre asked silently infiltrating my thought.

'She's fine — she's quite fine,' Dele said rapidly.

'Don't hide anything from me Dele — that's if you believe that I'm not out of my mind. I've being thinking about her all night. I stopped midway in my course of action because of her and the children, not to talk of the child inside her. To be honest with you, I first considered taking my own life, and I would have if not for Tinu and the children. I know the kids are safe at their nanny's, but Tinu — I'm even more scared now that she's not here...' Lanre said and broke down.

'Well Buroda, your God hasn't let you down at all. Mama Gbenga has been operated on and she and your daughter are doing fine at West-end hospital. We came straight here from there,' Dele explained.

'But ... but ... but ... she's only seven months pregnant...!' Dele stammered.

'Yes, seven months and a few days,' I completed speaking for the first time. 'And now Baba Gbenga you really have to pull yourself together. You've done so well up till now and we're all proud of you,' I stated, making sure not to address him as Dele so as not to ignite old animosity.

A moment's silence and then Lanre roared like a caged animal. A male nurse came to tell us that the visit was over. Like the expert he's been made to believe he is nothing we could say would convince him that Lanre was fine. The realisation that he'd made his own case worse also dawned on Lanre who sat there with clear eyes as if the bullish sound never emanated from him.

'Give her my love and regards Dele and Bunmi. Tell her

we'll be together again soon. We simply must get out of this hell,' Lanre whispered.

'Take good care Lanre,' I said utterly carried away.

Dele walked silently beside me. We avoided looking at each other for a while, and then I felt his eyes burning into me. I knew he was starring, and I've become quite familiar with his accusing stare where Lanre is concerned.

'You haven't stopped loving him — have you?' I heard him say.

'Yes! But it's you I'm married to,' I replied without thinking.

Six

'Bukola, do you know that Tunji has decided that he's going to put together the stories of our beginnings one day?' Bukola's mother said as soon as Bukola came into the room.

I looked embarrassed and certainly not as confident as I felt or sounded when I first spoke to Bukola's mother about the idea.

'In other words, he's going to be a writer and not a lawyer anymore. Where goes — Native Son — all that story about charging and bailing people who get jailed not because of what they've done but what they've said?' Bukola quizzed in return.

'There will be plenty others to do that,' I said carelessly.

'Oh! I see. So we're already into the politics and poetics of Otherness,' Bukola mused.

'More about poetics, I'll say. I can't see any politics in that. More of individual aptitude — I mean, what you're comfortable doing,' I replied.

'Comfortable! You certainly know how to choose your words. Comfort at whose expense? Here you are piecing together a societal tale — something that belongs to everyone, and you want it to lead you to a life of bliss and comfort,' Bukola fumed.

'You're just twisting whatever I said. Look I could have said confident — whatever you're confident doing if you like. I'm certainly not talking about living in a palace. But at least I'll need a roof over my head, and that of my family before I could begin to write,' I said.

'Same thing — confident! A trick — a confidence trick! Maami, this boy is deep — really deep. He has even chosen a wife and started pumping her full of kids. I'm sure he has even started fantasising about this new family unit — the shape and size of the wife who must not be fatter, taller or older than her man; she must first give birth to a baby boy or the heir apparent in the name of the Father, the Son, and whoever wants to come next!' Bukola ranted.

'Ma!' I cried: this girl is crazy, and that's why I didn't want

97

you to talk to her about the idea in the first place,' I said feeling embattled.

'Oh! I see — I can see that he's also not going to tolerate criticism of any kind.'

'I didn't say that!'

'What do you mean you didn't say that. Are there so many ways of saying that you detest your critics?' Bukola shouted.

'Well Tunji, have you started thinking about the structure or plot of your debut? Remember it's both inspiration and perspiration, and the former is only ten percent of what we're talking about I must warn you — the latter carries the rest,' Bukola's mother warned.

'I have actually, but I wouldn't like to talk about it in front of this cynic — she'll only snigger,' I said.

'You see there you have it — straight from the horse's snort. Our Baluban griot will only tolerate, nurse and nurture a coterie of acolytes who wouldn't dare raise a voice in dissent. Well, lets summarise the emerging creative scenario home boy: first, you appropriate a communal property — set yourself up in a not-too-comfortable home as you term it; beg, borrow or steal somebody's daughter; pump her full of kids; mummify or castrate your critics at home and abroad, and expect the human race to be grateful to you!' Bukola rounded.

'Now Bukola, when you get carried away, you really are something. What a way to kill the ten percent inspiration even before it's sprouted? Can you imagine a better way to document our plight other than putting it in black and white?' Bukola's mother said.

'Other than? I hate the word 'Other'. Once you mouth it, it triggers something in me — 'the Other' — that which can and must be exploited...'

'I certainly can see your point. But the word exists and must be put to rational usage. It has served a purpose in history which no one can deny, but it needs recontextualisation not banishment,' Bukola's mother said.

'My point precisely,' I said rediscovering my vocal cords. 'What the world needs — if I may borrow your defence of 'the Other' Ma — is recontextualisation and not banishment. We've all suffered abuses, degradation and oppression even from within our own culture. That's why I believe the starting point of any credible story will have to begin from the premise of the imperfections, divisions and conflicts from within — only with passing references to the agent provocateurs or catalysts from without — who motivated or brought these divisions into lesser or greater confusion. This part as a result of its aim to be factual rather than creative — must, of necessity, be tedious — or may appear so to many!' I said.

'You mean boring?' Bukola asked.

'May be,' I answered knowing that not answering her wouldn't help. 'But the second part would be more eclectic — more entertaining.'

'Meaning what? That you begin to distort the facts?' Bukola asked again.

'Not necessarily a distortion — more of a creative adaptation of your sources. And here you begin to teach, to impart, to entertain....'

'Meaning that you begin to mould people in your own image!' Bukola said before I could finish.

'It could be a combination of the two actually — factual and creative,' Bukola's mother said before I could say anything. 'In that second part I could contribute something I've filed away for quite some time. It's my critical plus creative response to our plight. I used to call it 'Our Redeemers Who Blurred their Minds'!' Bukola's mother said.

'You mean something lifted straight from the thesis? Now that's tedious!' Bukola yelled.

'May be not,' the mother replied smiling.

'Now I'm confused — totally confused. First, I thought we were talking about the giant ego of a Baluban griot or shall we say aspiring griot really. But it seems to be turning into something else — whose legs, whose arms à la Jacob? Or is it straightforwardly a communal masturbation in the erotic past?' Bukola fired.

'As you've said yourself — the story doesn't belong to an individual — it's a communal property or is there a better way to demonstrate that communality than to have a plural, I mean multiple voices in one tale?' I asked.

'That's right,' Bukola's mother said. 'Mine would merely supply the perspective of a generation — the older generation and how we've failed to regenerate.'

'Oh! that's perfect — just perfect. Now I get it. The cultural package — why don't we just describe the emerging critical plus creative scene as Gerontology Made Simple? Oba Ala must help us!' Bukola sniggered.

'Call it what you like, but I think we've done our very best to accommodate you,' I said jokingly.

'Accommodate? Did I hear you right? You see there you go refracting words again like you all do. One would have thought that I was a squatter daring to raise a voice at the AGM of the Council of Landlords!' Bukola replied.

'That's what you get when you constitute yourself into a nuisance — a pest,' I said still smiling: 'Why don't you contribute something — a cynical existentialist piece on the condition of man would do. Look Bukola, it's an evolving story and the eclectic section would easily ....'

'Thank you so much Mr. Chairman of the Censorship Board. I'm not headed in that direction at all — even then I take your offer of accommodation seriously — believe me I do. But I'll rather paddle my own canoe — as they say.'

'Disappointed. I am utterly disappointed. I thought you could do better than seeking refuge in cliché. But seriously, would this proverbial canoe be paddled strictly within a sniggering, manhating individualistic framework?' I teased.

'Yes! If you're talking about the cannibalistic kind eminently known and described as 'man-of-a-kind'. I'll keep to myself for as long as possible — does that bother you?' Bukola asked aggressively.

'Yes, as a matter of fact it does.'

'Why?'

'Because I happen to care — care about you much more than you know or appreciate.'

'Many thanks Atunda — father of knowledge! But when it comes to matters of belief I am a monolith....' Bukola stammered.

100

4. Once More With Passion: What Is Love?

One

'So what has changed?' Bukola asked.

'From what?' I replied

'From the days Chiefs used...!'

'...to sell their own people?' I completed, and we both burst out in derisive laughter.

'Nothing actually,' Bukola's mother said between hiccups and misty eyes: 'And we owe you children a lot of apologies. Many of us even thought that you would never be capable of understanding. Modern factorship was always going to be more vicious, more deadly than its older counterpart, and within that our own Middle-Passage had guessed, even anticipated its own end,' she said.

To which Bukola answered: 'But Maami, my question is, why take up their mode of apprehension in the first instance? Why fool yourself that you can ....'

'Out-manoeuvre them in their own game?' Bukola's mother asked. She answered her own question before either of us could speak: 'The answer is simple really. Remember what is said of the old Chief: 'It all started with the handkerchiefs...it was what the scarlet did for our people...when the Chiefs saw that the Whites — I think the Portuguese were the first — were taking out these scarlet handkerchiefs as if they were waving, they told the Blacks, 'Go on then and get scarlet handkerchiefs...And they were captured. The object is scarlet still — remodified and readapted. Scarlet peugeot. Scarlet radiogram — scarlet ford, scarlet this, scarlet that! While more charitable but no less racist authors went further to suggest that in times past and present the experience of slavery produced and still produces in us a sambo personality... essentially childlike in behaviour and character, a mental midget, a head-scratching, foot-shuffling over-grown child, grovelling and subservient to appetite...'

'Oh! I see your point Ma,' I said: 'Their postmodern equivalents must be having a field day understanding the neocolonial factors.'

'Only an extremist would deny the positive contributions to our social and political life made by the colonial enterprise — one of them wrote. They were ubiquitous, and deeply ingrained, far more so than any of us could imagine — he said. The education system alone opened up a cultural heritage that reached beyond Azania to Baluba and Timbuktu and Gao. It produced a highly developed tool with which a writer could explore his own unique predicament, just as the liberal traditions formed the basis for the struggle for independence from the colonial powers.'

'What a load of nonsense,' Bukola hissed.

'They know it to be so, but who can stop them? The same author even recognised the fact that the same tradition could be destructive. Petrified within the social structure, they could divide class from class, and constrict the evolution of national ways of life, he concluded. Precisely how one could view the division of class from class and the constriction of the evolution of national ways of life as being of equal advantage in a tradition whose only positive effect is the ability to provide an individual author with a highly developed tool of language with which to explore individual predicaments, beats me!'

'Welcome Sir!' Bukola and I said in unison. The man didn't even answer. He has been like that for days, possibly weeks now. News that Bukola's mother might leave her father has been topical in Olanibi street for some time now. Not a new phenomenon in Elizabethan island and among its uppitty denizens. 'The man and the woman simply grew apart; the spark in the relationship was gone; they just have to liberate themselves from the tyranny of marriage — the vows no longer seem to make sense, *et cetera, et cetera,*' are a few of the commonplace reasons often advanced to justify why a family ought to be ripped apart.

'Don't you think you should talk to him?' I asked Bukola.

'Who? Me? Who am I? You must be out of your mind to even suggest it. Look Tunji, I lost my father the day I rediscovered my mother. It's a paradox, isn't it?' Bukola said.

'But why does it have to be like that?' I asked really perturbed.

'I don't know. But it's true what they say about incompatibility. The two of them are utterly incompatible,' Bukola reiterated.

'How dare you say that? Look Bukola and Tunji, I really think that the two of you should maintain some respectable distance from this matter. I understand your concern. I appreciate it even. But Dele and I have been through this before, and he will come round,' Bukola's mother said from the other end of the living-room.

'Oh! I...we... I mean, we're sorry Ma,' I stammered.

'I know you didn't mean that I should hear you, and I'm sorry too if it appears like I've been eavesdropping. It's perfectly normal for you kids to talk about us, but I think you just don't get it,' she said.

'Oh? Is that what you really think? I don't want to say this too, and I apologise if it hurts your own feelings. But you don't know everything...!'

'Bukola, are you out of your mind? You really must stop now. Don't go on please,' I said hurriedly.

'Don't stop her Tunji. She really must be given a chance to express herself,' the mother counselled.

'Thank you Maami for conceeding that I deserve a say in this matter. But it's not just me, but also Michael and my sister who is not even anywhere near here to see how the two of you have been behaving lately!' Bukola blurted.

'So it's all my fault then?' Bukola's mother asked, and the pain in her voice was palpable.

'No! I didn't say that, and please don't let me say it Maami. We have gone through this a thousand times. Let me tell you for the umpteenth time — I am on your side. I feel your pain, and I love you more than words can ever express, but I also need my father. It is within your God-given power and ability to pull him back — to stop him from destroying himself!' Bukola said.

'Listen to me Bukola. You're an intelligent girl. I love you too, and I wish you a happy future. A future full of love and tenderness. I've said this before and would say it again. Perhaps for the last time I would want to ask once more with all the passion in me; what really is love? Is it when two human beings are united in greed, or as they say have chosen a way which appears right to them but in the end leads to destruction that we say they're in love? Bukola, what your father is asking is something that I've got but simply cannot give — my conscience. It's simply not for sale.'

'And I wouldn't even ask you to pay such a price simply to keep this family together. All I am saying is that you should try — try everything within your God-given power and the ability that I know you've got to convince him — I mean convert him to our common cause...' Bukola proffered.

'Thank you Bukola. But what we're up against here is the power of conviction — a deeply entrenched conviction in a way of life — a fanatical belief in a view of the world!' Bukola's mother said.

'I guess I know what you're talking about Maami. But shouldn't we also examine ourselves and our own set of beliefs? Are we also fanatical to a degree? And how much and to what degree are we prepared to shift within the prison-house of our own belief to accommodate some of the whims and caprices of the other side? Remember the injunction — wherever possible live peaceably with all men?' Bukola replied.

'Once again child, you've managed to answer your own question. Underline the keywords in that sound injunction that you've just mouthed — Wherever Possible! And please don't let me spell out all the possible angles of compromises that I've explored in this matter. I must admit that I'm close to giving up, but I'll like to assure you children that I wouldn't quit easily.'

With those words, Bukola's mother walked to the neat row of books on the shelves at the other end of the living-room. She picked up a pamphlet and walked slowly back towards Bukola and I, like a redoubtable Sunday School teacher reconstruc- ting a morality tale.

She said: 'Permit me to read to you a sermon which I read long ago and one which approximates — in my view — the injunction you've just quoted: The story concerns a boy who asked his dad, 'How do wars begin?' The father replied, 'Well, World War One began because Germany invaded Belgium.' At this point his wife interrupted, 'Tell the boy the truth. It began because somebody was murdered.' The husband quickly retorted, 'Are you answering the question or am I?' The wife stormed out of the room and slammed the door as hard as she could. When the room stopped vibrating, an uneasy silence followed. The son then said, 'Daddy, you don't have to tell me how wars begin. Now I know!" Bukola's mother set down the pamphlet and starred straight into our bleary eyes.

We could have laughed, but we didn't. The illogicality of war; the casualities of war; casualties who may, or may not be present when egos are inflated, or to put it in psychoanalytical terms — when the id reigned supreme in regions where the super-ego or at least the ego should have maintained control — suddenly hit Bukola and I. The mother sensed our reaction and in turn slumped on the sofa. The sofa received her featherweight with all the patience and capriciousness of a being used to being flogged: 'Don't stare at me like that Tunji — this thing can't breathe,' she said as if reading my thoughts.

'No Ma...!' I stammered, looking confused. 'I was merely thinking about wars and their illogicality,' I said.

'Well, I see what you mean. My uncle who went to the so-called Second World War epitomises the phenomena of wars. Along with one million others from this sick continent they were told to go and bleed for a cause they knew nothing about. But again, the real question remains how did it all began?' she asked.

'Because Hitler read Nietzsche, and...' Bukola began, but the mother waved her down.

'Don't repeat other people's line. Let me talk to you kids about my uncle. Let me tell you what that war did to him in spite of what Hitler did or may not have done. According to my father, he was a fine young man in his youth. A giant of the Osanyin lineage, and he was the one mostly favoured by my grandfather to bestow all his knowledge of our *orisa*! But the war came and he and thousands others were conscripted. They were drafted to fight in a war they knew nothing about. They formed what was called The King's African Riffle (KAR), and off they went to lands and climes where the King's interests — not an Ekiti king's — were badly threatened!'

It was getting dark and I had to bid Bukola and her mother farewell. At last my mother has dropped her fabled hostility to the imagined influence and indoctrination of Bukola and I by Bukola's mother. But the areas of conflict have merely deepened — herself and my father stoically on the side of Bukola's father in a war of attrition that may still claim several casualties. Bukola's mother reiterated daily that her major concerns were for the welfare of her three children. Bukola's older sister Olu had found a place for Bukola at her university in Europe, and in a matter of weeks, Bukola should embark on her voyage.

'Omo-Aiyeru pressurise your parents so that we can be together again soon,' Bukola said as I was getting ready to leave.

'I thought you were not supposed to care? Or have we dropped our fabled hostility to the cannibalistic kind known as 'man-of-a-kind'?' I asked in return.

'I would see to it that you leave together. This place isn't destined to get any better. Or let me put it this way, it's going to get a lot worse before...' Bukola's mother said.

'Oh! Don't be so pessimistic Maami. We can still beat this contemporary malaise at its own game. I promise we would!' Bukola responded.

'Yyes, you're our only hope — I mean both of you and your generation. Once you get it all wrong as we've done, then that is it — we're done for! Tunji, I want you to look after Bukola and her sister, and don't forget to work on that story of yours. I have given you my piece — haven't I? Just use it in any part of the story — don't even bother to acknowledge me, because the truth is that any member of my generation could have written that stuff,' Bukola's mother said sounding really old.

'I will try my best Ma', was all I could say, and Bukola stood up to walk me to the door. At the door we should have said goodnight, but instead Bukola came out and we strolled across the lawn into the early evening breeze. From the street we could hear the now more restful water of the Lagoon splattering against the banks a little over a mile away. Olanibi street and it's neat row of houses with their curtains drawn — appeared equally restive. Bukola held my hand as we walked in the middle of the deserted asphalt road.

'What do you think is going to happen here — I mean in this land with all the morbid posturings going on right now?' Bukola asked.

'I wish I knew. But as your mother said, I think it's going to get a lot worse before it gets any better!' I said feeling tight within me.

'But does it really have to be like that? It's like a death-wish isn't it, and no one appears set or determined to avert it.'

'I think you're right. Looking at the micro as well as macro levels this society would still tear itself apart a bit more before....!'

'Don't even say it Omo-Aiyeru! I've heard that refrain too many times, it's making me giddy!' Bukola responded before I could even finish.

'You better go back, otherwise I'll have to walk you back again,' I said, and we both laughed at how many times that had happened.

'Oh! Not the *ikokò* story again Tunji,' Bukola said sounding lighthearted.

'Okay then, you better go back,' I replied.

'Not until you've promised to... Oh! Never mind!'

'Promise what?' I asked really baffled.

'To give what my mother said a thought. I know you would rather stay here in Baluba and struggle through thick and thin to finish your education. But Tunji, Olu and I would need you, and I in particular would definitely appreciate your company and comraderie in taking care of the obsfuscated lot over there.'

'Don't call people you haven't met names,' I said lightly, drawing Bukola close to me. She rested her pretty head on my shoulder, and I scratched her closely shaven kinky hair tickling her scalp: 'Why don't you let your hair grow and then do terrible things to it — like all civilised women do? Your hair is so short I swear to God I can smell your brains!' I said again.

'Now who's repeating other people's lines? Go on then black boy and don't try to make me shame! But please Tunji could we try to rise above all that right now?'

'And do what?' I asked.

'Talk about things that matter.'

'Such as?'

'Giving me a straight forward answer to my request', Bukola replied unabashedly.

'I don't know Bukola — I really don't know. I may join you, I'll love to join you — is all I could say at this moment.'

'Well, thanks for being so caring' Bukola responded, sounding hurt.

'But this Middle-Passage thing!' I sighed.

'What about it?' Bukola asked.

'I don't mean to sound tedious but I just can't believe it's happening to us all over again.'

'Oh! You mean the three generations analogy?' Bukola stated.

'Precisely!'

'Consider it as the story of the intractable or protracted battle between the dress and the lice. Unless the one eliminates the other, the innocent finger-nails would continue to be bloodied!' Bukola explained again.

'I'm afraid you're right. But who's the 'I' and who is the 'Other'? From being God's Bits of Wood, have we been reduced to mere finger-nails? I asked.

'The terms need rehabilitation not banishment,' Bukola replied, and chuckled at the reflexive, rebounding irony.

108

'Okay! Okay! Okay! You win!' I said.

'So what do you say then?' Bukola asked earnestly.

'I will give the matter some serious thought — that's all I can say for now'.

'That's enough for me Omo-Aiyeru, and many thanks!' Bukola responded — kissing me lightly on the cheek.

'Goodnight' I said, holding her hands in mine.

'Sleep well Tunji'

'See you in the morning,' I said releasing Bukola's hands and patting her on the shoulders!

The air was feverish at the airport on the day of our departure. Neocolonial angst has since begun to prove a lethal combination with zero-hearted decolonisation, and the Baluban clime is reeling. Many trappings — or what were considered to be trappings of nationhood — have since produced catalytic results. Paradigmatic things have not simply fallen apart but have turned out — you might say — just the ways the designers of this culpable world would rather have it. The army which was meant to defend a nation became a law unto itself — leaving us with two giant parties of politics — the membership of the one largely drawn from the army and the enigmatic other comprising largely of the rest of us! The large number of surprised millionaires looking at the rest of us surprised came from the former, and leaders of the latter amounted to bootlickers and eaters of military leftovers. The topical issues of the day centered around how we came about an army before we've had a nation; an army many reasoned was supposed to defend a nation — a sovereign nation — and not this ill-defined, ill-theorised entity called Baluba.

My mother held baby Adebowale to her chest as she discussed with Bukola's mother the changes that have occurred in voyaging from the outposts to the metropolis within the last twenty years. As usual, the one spoke in ephemeral terms — the other was philosophical. Within the past twenty years, the Baluban Airways flight 007 or what many have begun to refer euphemistically as the Baluban Airwaste, has also replaced the Elder Debska of our parents' sojourn. Twenty years ago the journey lasted fifteen whole days, but today it takes a mere six hours to reach the metropolis:

'Ten years from now, it would be five hundred years since Columbus's voyage, and we're still stunk in stupor!' Bukola's mother said.

'No we're not,' my mother disagreed: 'look at all the progress we have made. Seventeen years ago, when I was embarking on the same voyage, my own mother didn't even know the way to Port-city. But there you are — you and I — sending and seeing these kids off!'

'But that's neither here nor there', Bukola's mother replied: 'Just look at the antics that accompany the voyage today,' she said pointing at our sweaty fathers, and their struggles to secure boarding-passes for Bukola and I.

The antics were frantic, and having read how she described our need for an awakening that would probably never come in 'Our Redeemers,' I knew what Bukola's mother was talking about. I remember my own anger as I stood at the Port eight years ago to welcome my own parents after nine and ten years of sojourn. My mind went back to Aiyeru and the changes that have occurred there too since the returnee's return. Since the over-orchestrated boom that propelled Baluba — in the imagination of its leaders — into the middle ranks of developed nation — the sojourn has become rather routine, and it's probably goodriddance, I thought, that no welcoming party — like this low key farewell — would ever be as grand as what my father received in Aiyeru seven years ago. Before she left for where all elders must go ultimately, Maami-Agba had assembled all her children — including us grand and a handful of great-grandchildren — again. She reminded them of the need to strike a balance always between history, tradition and religion: 'Don't subsume any aspect of your heritages — contemporary or otherwise — your cosmic apprehension,' she called it, 'because whatever you subsume doesn't go away. It lurks there somewhere in your subconscious and you've got to know how to deal with it', she reminded them. Aiyeru partied after she was gone, but the balance she cherished was hardly upheld or given a moment's thought.

110

Tradition fought religion and hardly was anyone able or willing to inject a sense of history into an event that cried for one. The traditionalists spoke in rigid terms and the protestant-hosannas sang themselves hoarse condemning them.

I hardly noticed that our fathers had rejoined us — clutching the boarding passes as if they were purchased with blood. Bukola who held my left hand in her right shook me awake. I awoke in time to hear my mother say something about not being a dreamer and the need to be clear headed in the metropolis. It was time to say goodbye, and my eyes were misty. Ralph, Liz and Mike the destroyer had been summoned by Bukola's father from the airport gallery to come and bid Bukola and I farewell for now. I took six month old baby Adebowale from my mother without knowing what I was doing. The words popped out before I'd had time to structure my thoughts: 'I certainly hope little fellow that when it's your turn Baluba would be able to provide all the education that you'll need,' I said, kissing him lightly on the lips before giving him back to my mother. I shook Ralph's hands and asked him to take care of himself and everyone else. He said he would and everyone laughed. I turned to Liz who was struggling with her tight fitting jeans. She leaned heavily on Mike the destroyer who was holding Bukola's hands. Bukola patted both of them on the shoulder and I did the same.

'Well, you've got to go,' Bukola's mother said as if making an important announcement: 'Olu must be waiting for you at the other end, and you must remember to write, the moment you touch down.'

'The daughter-of-a-bird soaring in the clear blue sky!' my father hailed Bukola, and we all laughed. Bukola smiled and courtesied at him and her smiling father. My father touched me lightly on the head, and our eyes locked for a split second. I clutched my hand luggage and moved shoulder to shoulder with Bukola towards the immigration barriers. After the first set of railings, we looked back to bid the families a final farewell. Fathers and mothers as well as our brothers and sister waved frantically as if their entire lives depended on it. The flight was on schedule, and in six hours, we would be

confronted with our own Middle-Passage, I thought bitterly.
The immigration officer scrutinised Bukola's passport and visa
— then mine — and waved us on. The custom officers fussed
over our hand luggages. They asked a multitude of questions
— ranging from what we were carrying in our bags to how
much local and foreign currencies we were taking with us.

> — Lets count the truths, ancient one!
> For is it true that we were grandly absent when they
> soared aloft
> In anno Domini 1783 with the hot-air balloon that is
> the ancestor of the supersonic jet of today.
> Yes, it is true that the SST and the 777 have arrived
> and the space shuttle is rocketed into orbit
> assisted by seven million pounds of thrust — sheer
> thrust!

I moaned once settled in the comfy seat of the Boeing 777.
Bukola asked what that was, and I mumbled something about
'one race's quarrel against another's gods!'

'You're certainly not going to dream your way through the
next six hours! Look Tunji, I know you never desired this
sojourn, but since we're here why don't we share our thoughts
instead of mumbling at each other?' Bukola asked seemingly
perplexed.

'Alright, shoot!' I said, sitting bold upright to confront her
bleary eyes.

'Just stay awake,' she said tickling the palm of my left hand
affectionately.

I tried to look into her eyes, but she'd rested her head on my
shoulder, and I in turn closed my eyes. 'Who would have
thought that the same fate would befall us so soon?' Bukola
mused.

'I thought we've just agree that no one is allowed to dream
for the next six hours daughter-of-a-bird soaring...?' I
stuttered, as the giant Boeing taxied and soared. The jet was
half full, and Bukola and I had a three seater to ourselves. As
the jet dominated the Baluban sky — indeed conquering it! —
the Atlantic coast became visible. Images of crossing and

re-crossing surged in my mind. I remembered Bukola's mother's apt description of those images: 'Would we be counted among the lucky ones who are able to recross this Passage-of-dispossession — or numbered among the multitude who wouldn't dare — not out of choice but out of compulsion as our mother puts it — to return!' I said to myself or so I thought.

'We shall see — we would certainly see!' Bukola replied, and I was jolted. 'Well, welcome back to the land of the living native son. I know you never meant to be audible, but that's the nature of somnambulists — they often puke in the hot-house of neocolonial angst — without knowing it of course!' Bukola said and smiled at me.

Part Three

The European states achieved national unity at a moment when the national middle classes had concentrated most of the wealth in their hands. Shopkeepers and artisans, clerks and bankers monopolised finance, trade and science in the national framework. The middle class was the most dynamic and prosperous of all classes. Its coming to power enabled it to undertake certain very important speculations: industrialization, the development of communications and soon the search for outlets overseas.

In Europe, apart from certain slight differences (England, for example, was some way ahead), the various states were at a more or less uniform stage economically when they achieved national unity. There was no nation which by reason of the character of its development and evolution caused affront to the other.

Today, national independence and growth of national feeling in under-developed regions take on totally new aspects.

(Frantz Fanon, *The Wretched of the Earth*)

Whether the fight is painful, quick or inevitable, muscular action must substitute itself for concepts.

(Frantz Fanon, *The Wretched of the Earth*)

5. The Auction Bloc

One

No one, living or dead, could say when this dispersal began. Like seeds — to disperse is to contribute to a milieu — to advance the cause of a system — an eco-system. In the spirit of our ancestors and their belief that the world is a masquerade — we've dispersed voluntarily and forcibly in times past and present. But in ecological terms — the present dispersal is a disaster — a grim, unmitigated ecological disaster:

> *We bleed for your race's sake!*
> *We're here for your race's sake*
> *We make your dreams come true!*
> *Every mess you make*
> *Every single mess you make*
> *Shall be cleaned by us!*

We appear to be singing day and night. I repeated the refrain in my head as the lengthy escalator moved interminably. But hasn't it been said and must be constantly brought to remembrance — that three generations cannot — must not revel in poverty? Spiritual poverty — mind you — which is far more dangerous and catastrophic than its material counterpart — is what the departed ancestors warned us about. In 'Our Redeemers', didn't Bukola's mother remind us that when our energy is consumed with material this and that — when we concentrate our mental and physical prowess into building a˙house, and neglect the weighty issue of building the character of our children — isn't it certain that it is the unbuilt

116

children that would destroy the house that we are struggling so hard to build?

Bukola and Olu were waiting for me at the other end of the lengthy escalator. We meet here every morning to go to our first early morning job. The first of three jobs interspersed with our classes on different campuses within this vast European city. At different hours of the day we went to this or that other job to supplement our meagre earnings, and in the process keep body and soul together. The ordeal require planning — careful planning. Lectures must not interfere with work and vice versa.

'So what time did you go to bed last night Omo-Aiyeru?,' Bukola asked as I shook hands with her and her sister.

'Well, I'm nearly through now with the first part of *The Dancing Masquerade*,' I said, but Bukola wasn't quite pleased.

'When would you learn to answer questions straight without...! I asked you a straightforward question. The question once again — Omo-Aiyeru — is when you went to bed last night,' Bukola fired back.

'I think I've answered your question, and if you hadn't interrupted I would have done better. But you see...'

'Oh! You two, please don't start again — it's just too early in the day. You've got the rest of the day mind you to continue your eternal wrangling!' Olu interjected.

'Many thanks elder sister. But you see this girl is just insufferable,' I replied jokingly.

'And who may I ask is this girl? I'm also your elder you know, or is that what this *Ilu Oyinbo* has turned us into?' Bukola queried.

'You know that's an argument no one is likely to win. And as elder sister Olu said, it's really too early in the day for such a morbid topic,' I said.

'Oh! I see, so instead of you to learn some manners, you think you can scare us with the fear of death?' Bukola persisted.

'Oh! Isn't that great Bukola — now who is the Christ of the apocalypse, or to put it mildly who between you and I is the *Jesu Oyingbo*?'

'Now you two had better put a stop to this. You know that

Tom Fisher will just like to fire both your asses from this job, and you know what that means to your existence, don't you?' Olu warned.

Tom Fisher is the untrained, uneducated supervisor cum proud owner of the cleaning company employed by the *IPF* magazine. All the giant magazine establishment wants is to have its desks, fifteen floors and a bewildering array of manual and electric typewriters, and other equipments cleaned and polished before the workers resume their daily activities. We've got two hours to ourselves to do just that. Tom Fisher inherited the company from his mother twenty years ago, who in turn inherited it from her own father thirty years before Tom was born. The only improvement Tom has brought into the outfit is the new name — Office Dusters! Now with endless supply of cheap black and brown labour, Tom reckons that the company has entered the golden age of its prosperity. 'Come rain or shine', Tom Fisher has been heard to have mouthed, 'I expect my cleaners in by half past five'. Endless lines of willing hands trudging in daily to ask if there were vacancies has made us dub the place the Auction Bloc of the late twentieth century, and Tom isn't alone. 'The cleaning industry is worth millions,' Tom mouthed often enough. To whom the millions went is quite a different story altogether. We were expected to behave like clean little boys and girls, and that is all. Ask Tom a question that made him think, and you risk being fired. The era of illegal immigrants, employing all sorts of disingenuous tactics to reach the European metropolis meant that Tom, and his cohorts in the cleaning industry (the very name makes you want to puke — doesn't it?), held all the aces. The more illegal they are, the more docile and subservient they are guaranteed to remain. And Tom simply loved it all. Baluban youths and young adults and others from the subcontinent whose lives have been decimated by decades of home rule — a phenomenon that has proved thus far to be more vicious and far more deadly than colonial rule — escaped more and more — to seek God alone knows what!

Those of us who were qualified to do other things — such as elder sister Olu Osanyin — tried their luck, and were returned in a variety of ways back to the cleaning industry.

'You see, we cannot give you a job permit, Dr. Osanyin, if you don't have a job,' elder sister Olu was told at the Home Office.

Believing that to be true, Olu went feverishly after a job. She applied for everything. Her credential was perfect. With a thesis in Social Anthropology that did not merely revise, but actually rewrote the received image of a number of Black cultures, she was shortlisted — at least for interview — for every job to which she applied. Many shortlisted her out of curiosity, and others out of genuine interest. Using the ideas and opinions of a variety of scholars from a variety of fields and disciplines — most especially those who have attacked the imperialism of Western cultures from within — she made it clear in her thesis, and before her examiners that she didn't have to invent anything — she merely transcribed. Finally, Olu got two jobs — or to be precise two half-jobs — making one, isn't it? She signed the contracts for the two jobs, and ran to the Home Office with that 'Got ya!' look on her face.

'Why did you apply for these jobs?' she was asked by the same Home Office functionary who told her that they wouldn't give her a permit unless she had a job.

'Because I needed them,' she replied simply.

'Oh! You don't seem to understand my question,' the functionary explained slightly irritated.

'What part of your question don't I understand?' Olu wanted to know.

'That you were not supposed to apply for those jobs!' the man said without emotion.

'I see. So how am I expected to survive, if I don't have a job?' Olu wanted to know.

Anger and fury now showed on the man's face, but he did his best not to answer angrily. The grim nature of their preternaturally predetermined roles in the whole affair occurred to both Olu and her tormentor at different times and in varying degrees during the one sided interview.

'Remember what you told me the last time I came to apply for a work permit?' Olu finally asked the slightly flustered functionary.

'Yes! Yes! Yes! I remember. That's what the GO said, and I

didn't invent it you know'.

'*Stimmt!*' Olu replied.

'What was that?'

'I said that was Perfect.'

'That's what I thought it was, but you're not allowed to speak in a foreign language here, you know,' the man said really angry.

'And do you know what language that was?' Olu asked the bewildered functionary.

'It sounded familiar, but I really don't care — it's foreign! — and that's all that matters. And please let me make it clear to you once again that you don't do the questioning here. You haven't come here to teach us our job. If you have nothing else to say — good morning! Dr. Osanyin,' the man said with banality.

Olu was already gathering the papers of her two jobs when another bespectacled pencil-like man walked into the room. Looking through the glass partition through which Olu and her tormentor had been brow beating one another, the pencil-like man with his equally pencil-like rimmed spectacle looked oddly familiar. Olu dismissed the thought of the man's familiarity from her mind immediately.

'Hey! I've seen you somewhere before,' the man exclaimed from behind the glass partition. 'The name is Mike Ridgeway, and what can we do to help?' the thin man asked.

'I am Dr. Olubunmi Osanyin Jnr, and your colleague has spelt out in unambiguous terms that I'm here on an impossible mission,' Olu replied.

'And what would that mission be?' the man wanted to know.

'She's here to apply for a job permit. But according to the GO she shouldn't have applied for a job in the first place,' the functionary replied before Olu could speak.

'You see, there you have it straight from the General Order. The last time I was here, this same man told me that I can't have a permit unless I have a job. But today, I've signed contracts for two part-time jobs at two of your nation's top institutions and I still can't have a permit,' Olu responded finally.

'What those institutions did was illegal, and we are going to write to them. They will be well punished — believe me!' the functionary replied.

'Punished for what? They interviewed me along with other candidates you know? I believe that they offered me these jobs based on my qualification and suitability, or doesn't that figure in your scale of punishment in any way,' Olu queried.

His eyes increasingly fidgety and amused while dashing from the man next to him behind the glass partition to the lionised woman on the other side, whom he was still convinced he'd seen somewhere before, Mike Ridgeway finally intervened: 'May I see those papers?' Mike Ridgeway suggested, extending his thin hands towards the potlike hole created for the sole purpose of exchanging papers between the tormentor and the tormented. 'You should have referred the matter to me Mr. Bottomley,' Mike Ridgeway said to the man beside him, at the same time as his hands touched Olu's over-scrutinised papers.

'I thought it was a rather straightforward matter Dr. Ridgeway. I'd read the GO well, and section four, sub-section three says that a foreigner may not...!'

'Yes! Yes! Yes! I know what section four, sub-section three says, but you should have referred the case to me all the same. Only a head of section has got the final say on such an application — you know?' Ridgeway said menacingly.

'I know that Dr. Ridgeway. I only thought that there was no point wasting your time over something like that!' the now defensive Bottomley replied.

'Excuse me Dr. Osanyin! As you can see I'm only just hearing about this for the first time. Would you please wait in the reception area while I take a look at these papers? I promise not to keep you longer than necessary,' Mike Ridgeway explained.

'Please feel free to waste your time as he says. I can see that you are well meaning, but the GO is what you are struggling against,' Olu said feeling rather bemused.

Ron Bottomley shot Olu that may-I-never-see-you-again look. The import wasn't lost on Olu who replied under her breath that the feeling was mutual. 'These are the same men whose ancestors scrambled for and partitioned my continent barely a century ago — leaving us with funny and meaningless names such as Baluba — meaning the people who live around the Baluba river — now hiding behind glass partitions to read out rules that were non-existent when their ancestors trampled the earth. Yes, the feeling is mutual' — Olu swore again. She picked up her top-coat, hat and bag and walked out of the cubicle she'd been for the past two hours. Out in the reception area, Ron Bottomley's buzzer came alive and two visibly nervous black women and a man walked in together. 'One of those!' — Olu muttered to herself again!

Thoughts of this and that crowded her mind as Olu took one of the seats vacated by the trio of two nervous women and their man. The outcome of the trip to the Home Office would certainly affect the direction of her life one way or the other. From murderous thoughts towards their father who, according to report, has gone virtually berserk back home in Baluba, Olu thought bitterly about the plight of a mother she has not seen for close to eight years now. Bukola's father is now the quintessential Elizabethan Island socialite, and renowned patron of several of the rag-tag, artless Juju bands mushrooming all over Port-City! Of course, we all knew that the spark in their relationship was long gone. Since the days of her alleged indoctrination of Bukola and I, Bukola's mother had been subjected to ceaseless and increasing persecution by both the immediate family of her husband — championed by no less a figure than the Ekiti-witch of her primordial distaste and the equally obfuscated vicious circle in which the husband socialised. She could only watch in despair as the man she married degenerated from a fun loving socialite to a serial lover, and rumours have it that he'd fathered a number of children here and there. Of course, the whole thing was sweet music to the ears of lady mother-in-law who had never stopped nagging her daughter-in-law to give her more grand-children than the three she had produced thus far. Bukola's mother soon had to move out of their Elizabethan Island home, to a far more ordinary part of the fast moving city. She made the education of her children her sole goal. Long after the husband had stopped funding the education of his children at home and abroad, Bukola's mother taxed herself relentlessly to keep them in school. Her unfinished thesis in Social Anthropology became Olu's lot. As she continued in her painful remembrance, Olu didn't notice Mike Ridgeway, smiling rather benignly as he approached her in the reception area.

'A penny for your thoughts,' Ridgeway said as he approached.

Looking up, Olu saw the thin man towering above her, briefcase, hat and topcoat in hand. 'Yes, it's breaktime, and I thought I could explain a few things to you — unofficially that is — if you allow me — over coffee,' Ridgeway muttered nervously.

'And why would you want to do that?' Olu asked visibly angry and suspicious.

'Because I would like to. As I said, I've seen you somewhere before. I was also at Northbank University you know?'

'So, why should that surprise me? My race was badly outnumbered at Northbank,' Olu replied.

'Can't we try to rise above race? Wouldn't my race be outnumbered in Baluba if this encounter were to be taking place there?' Ridgeway asked in return.

'*Stimmt!*' Olu said in reply.

'I can see that you've been trampling my continent as well,' Ridgeway said playfully.

'Does that bother you? Or should I be apologising as I did to your brother in there?' Olu queried, pointing at the door to Bottomley's torture chamber.

'Oh! I see, Ron must have read you the riot act — I suppose.'

'So what did you do at Northbank, since you have had the good fortune of checking my entire life even before I'm able to know a thing about you? You see, the playing field is never level between you and I, and I doubt if it will ever be,' Olu said bitterly.

'I wrote a thesis on the consumerist aspect of information technology,' Ridgeway replied almost apologetically. The bitterness in Olu's voice was certainly not lost on him.

'Meaning that you studied the behaviour of innocent beings who were not even aware that you were examining their private life. Anyway Dr. Ridgeway, it's really kind of you to want to explain things to me unofficially, but I really don't see the point of that.'

'Please call me Mike. My favourite café is just two blocks from here, and at least let us have coffee together, before you rush off,' Mike Ridgeway offered.

'If you insist on wasting your time, I guess I really can't stop you. I've got about an hour to kill. If you refuse me permit for these jobs, I've got to think also about the implications of that for my life. I can't continue cleaning offices and toilets to survive you know?' Olu said matter-of-factly.

'I haven't said that we're refusing you anything. I only said that I'll like to know you better and explain one or two things to you over coffee,' Ridgeway responded.

'No! That wasn't what you said. And how did that bit about knowing me better come into the configuration? I thought we were only explaining things from a liberal humanist perspective to the sickeningly ideological — albeit from the coloniser to the colonised?' Olu proferred.

Ridgeway smiled in spite of himself. Olu rose to her feet, and they both walked into the winter afternoon. Ridgeway hailed an empty black cab, held the back door for Olu and climbed in beside her. Ten minutes later, they walked into a café swarming with early afternoon lunchers. Mike Rigdeway picked two menu lists as he led the way to a table for two beside the northern window in the café overlooking the busy street. He extended his hand to take Olu's coat, and she muttered her thanks as she handed it to him. Once seated, Olu examined the menu and made up her mind to stick to coffee, and snacks. But Mike Ridgeway had other ideas. The café, he announced happily, served the best fish and chips in town, and he offered to pay Olu back in the unlikely case that she was disappointed. The thought of food made her realise that she had had time for only a cup of coffee before leaving for the Home Office. Of course, her day began at five o'clock as usual. The two hour cleaning job at *IPF* magazine had become a permanent mainstay of our survival for so long. The two hour labour at the auction bloc guarantees payment of rent and travel cards for the week. After that you could then make a dash for something else as Olu did this morning. Inside the café, the orders were placed and Olu and Mike both sipped their coffee in silence.

Olu said finally: 'You really don't have to do this, you know? But I appreciate it — I really do. Gestures like yours assures one that there's still some hope for the human race after all! Sorry your brother irritated me a bit, but I have no right to take that out on you.'

'Oh, come on Olu! I know how ignorant his type could be, and that's why I have offered to explain one or two things to you. I was serious when I said I had seen you somewhere before.'

Two

But Bukola introduced the whole idea as a scandal. 'What do you mean a scandal is brewing between our sister and the Home Office?' I asked at the other end of the telephone line.

'Look here Omo-Aiyeru, I know a scandal — at least a potential scandal! — when I smell one,' Bukola responded.

'Bukola, there is a world of difference between a full blown scandal, and a story that has the potential of developing into one. The difference, lest you've forgotten or don't even know is that not all such stories ever achieve their full potentiality!' I screamed.

'Okay, okay! I see your point. But are you going to get over here and examine this situation before it achieves its full potentiality as you've surmised — Atunda?'

I smiled. Knowing that Bukola has characteristically given the story her own twist and spin. But the story of an Home Office functionary who should have grilled the life out of elder sister Olu as they are wont to, now coming to dinner at Olu's and Bukola's was certainly intriguing. I giggled into the mouthpiece: 'Did you say that our sister practically seduced the man, or whose move was it?'

'Hey, you sacrilegious griot — or aspiring griot really — are you coming or not? I've told you all that you need to know for now, and if you're ever going to make it as a recorder of socio-cultural this and that, you've got to develop a nose for societal scandals!'

'Wrong again. Grioting is not about scandals! Before cultures clashed and classes were constricted against class, and the evolutions of national...'

'Yesss! Yes! Don't read me the entire credo — I've got it,' Bukola chipped in before I could finish.

From the East End to the South West of the city where Bukola and Olu lived, took me the best part of an hour to travel given the light weekend traffic. Several tube stations

126

and two bus rides and at last I rapped on the door to their housing estate flat. I had struggled between bringing with me on the journey extracts of *The Dancing Masquerade* needing review and revision, but finally decided to do something more pleasurable. Now here I was clutching the paper back edition of my favourite African-American tale, *Invisible Man*. The story of a man almost killed by a phantom came to my mind, and the refrain Apologise! Apologise! sang in my head. Olu yanked the door opened, and her mood changed from utter surprise to affectionate love as she beheld my fragile frame.

'Greetings,' I said. 'May I come in?'

'Come in Tunji. Did Bukola know you were coming? She just went out to fetch some groceries,' Olu replied innocently.

'So it's true then?' I asked stupidly.

'What is true?'

'That...that...Oh! Never mind. I'll just wait until Bukola comes,' I said.

'Now Tunji, before I throw you out of this dingy flat, just tell me what you two have been gossiping about,' Olu replied, rather bemused. Somehow I had a feeling that she knew what her sister had been up to.

'No, I can't. I just can't. That would amount to a betrayal,' I said.

'Betrayal of who — if I may ask?'

'A trusted friend,' I replied.

'My mind tells me to ignore the two of you completely and pray that you both die in your contrite mischief...' Olu said lightly.

'Oh! You mean like Elegbara standing before Oba-Ala's hut reeking of...'

'Exactly. You've got the picture, and may Osumare provide the tricolour...'

'No, no, no! elder sister a full blown rainbow would do,' I completed for her. 'And as Alasofunfun reminded Elegbara when he dared pour derision on a palaeolithic medium — 'that may I remind you is the very stuff on which civilizations are built," I raved in a guttural voice.

'Somehow, I feel like forgiving you — both of you — for you

seem not to know what you're doing.'

'Oh! That is certainly scriptural. But remember that our struggle is not against flesh and blood!' I said also lightly. The turn of the key on the main door signalled Bukola's arrival. Olu's gaze and mine blazed the entrance. Bukola took her time, setting down her bag of groceries and taking off her coat before entering the living room.

'Omo-Aiyeru, what brings you to this part of the town? I thought East-Enders are fiercely proud of their roots, and would rather not mix with the multicultural world — just yet!' Bukola said feigning surprise.

'You invited him — didn't you? Oh, I hate you' Olu said before I could answer.

'What is she on about — Omo Aiyeru? How long have you been here, and what have you two being talking about behind my back?'

'Well, I don't believe in dilly-dallying you see. If a full blown scandal is about to erupt between us and the Home Office — our veritable hosts! — I suppose I've got the historic responsibility to stop the whole thing from becoming a diplomatic row,' I said.

'Your sense of history is certainly misplaced, and whoever put you up to it is even sicker than you. The two of you ought to be locked up in that giant asylum in the East-End,' Olu replied feigning severe anger.

'Okay, calm down both of you. Tunji, you've managed to blow it again — haven't you? You were asked to witness *gobi*, and the way you've gone about poking *gobi-gobi*? I fear for you — you know?' Bukola rounded on me.

'And what about the speck in your own eyes? Whose idea was it anyway, and now to behold you playing Mother Teresa! I'm sick of the two of you,' Olu said. She went into the kitchen slamming the door so hard behind her. Bukola and I stared hard at each other. The blow was perfectly aimed, and my sixth sense had told me to expect it. I caught Bukola's fist in my open palm and the full impact of her resultant loss of balance sent both of us reeling on the carpeted floor.

'But how can you let the cat out of the bag so early?' Bukola asked, still panting on top of me on the floor.

'It wasn't my fault. She suspected the moment I arrived. But when is he arriving?' I asked in return.

'Any time from now — I suppose. Look I've told Olu not to be so vindictive. She appears set to murder the guy. I mean, she's prepared a giant dish of fresh fish pepper soup more fit for the Alayeru just recovering from a deadly flu than a fragile Home Office functionary. Apparently the guy had known my sister at Northbank University, and had probably being a secret admirer...' Bukola rallied on.

'Hey! Take it easy,' I said: 'You've probably got it all wrong. The fellow could be well meaning — you know?'

'*Siddon* there!' Bukola replied: 'Anyway the reason why I've summoned you here is purely for self defence. Once I take a look at the guy and I don't like him, I want you to take him out at once. This is Baluban soil — you know — and he has no right being here in the first place. Anything would do — and I don't give a damn about diplomacy'.

'So you think that the taxi driver stuff that you're recommending would solve the problem? And when did this become the Baluban embassy in Carthage?' I asked.

'Look here Tunji, our sovereignty amounts to nothing. That's what gives this Northbank fellow the audacity to assume too much. And if all those ingrates at the Baluban House don't know what to do, you and I owe it to our people to see that our independence of mind and spirit is not always violated. I'm here to see how culpable my sister happens to be in the whole ordeal, and I intend to be objective — you know?'

The door bell rang as Bukola completed her remarks. We stood transfixed as if a bolt of lightening had just travelled through the room. Olu came out of the kitchen, looked from Bukola to me — the contempt in her eyes, plain and undisguised. We braced ourselves for the inevitable as Olu and Mike conversed briefly in the patio before coming into the living-room. Mike still clutched the parcel he had with him as he came into the living-room. He starred from Bukola to me, muttering a polite hello.

'This is my sister Bukola, and our brother Tunji,' Olu said: 'They're both here to see to it that you don't rape me before, during or after dinner.'

Mike laughed ruefully: 'Oh! I've heard so much about the two of you, and I'm so pleased to meet you. Is Tunji *our* brother in the sense in which all Balubans are brothers and sisters?' Mike asked.

'I'll advice you to avoid clichés and stereotypes tonight Mike — at least when dealing with these two. It just wouldn't help you at all. Don't believe anything they say either. The truth is that they're not pleased to see you. Sit down and don't say too much. You're in enemy's territory — you have been warned,' Olu replied.

But Mike stood his ground. He had come — it seems — to be as free as possible. Bukola extended her hand, and muttered how pleased she was to meet Mike at last. She deliberately turned her back on me so that I couldn't see her face. Mike in turn grasped the proferred hand, and said it was his pleasure to meet her. I had little choice but to follow suit. Olu came out again from the kitchen, and announced that dinner would be ready in fifteen minutes. Bukola seized the opportunity to inform Mike and I that she will have to go and give her sister a helping hand. It seems my historic responsibility had begun earlier than I expected. Another living-ancestor's negritudian piece raced through my mind, complementing the *Invisible Man*'s quasi-philosophical attitude of overcoming them with yesses!

> So I have learned many things son!
> I have learned to wear many faces
> like dresses — homeface,
> officeface, streetface, hostface, cock-
> tailface, with all their conforming smiles
> like a fixed portrait smile
>
> And I have learned too
> to laugh with only my teeth
> and shake hands without my heart.
> I have also learned to say 'Goodbye,'
> when I mean 'Goodriddance':
> To say 'Glad to meet you'

130

without being glad; and to say 'it's been
nice talking to you,' after being bored.

But believe me, son
I want to be what I used to be
when I was like you. I want
to unlearn all these muting things.
Most of all, I want to relearn
how to laugh, for my laugh in the mirror
shows only my teeth like a snake's bare fangs!

The ancestor had written. The philosophy of negritude —
according to the living-ancestor-griot who had undertaken the
most up-to-date revision of it — should never be belittled!
What went wrong with it was the socio-racial direction which
governed a whole literary ideology and gave it its choice of
mode of expression and thematic emphasis!

'So what are you doing in my country, Tonje?' Mike asked as
I continued in my reverie. Faces appeared in my mind —
Hostface! Homeface! Cocktailface! *et al,* — and I dismissed
them in the order of their appearance.

'Oh, I'm just putting finishing touches to my first full length
novel,' I said carelessly.

'Olu never told me that you were a writer.'

'An aspiring writer really,' I corrected.

'And what is your novel about?' Mike asked.

'It's an ethnobiography.'

'You mean the biography of an ethnic group — your ethnic
group?'

'*Genug!*'

'Oh! So Olu is not the only one who has trampled my
continent!' Mike stated again. I laughed, but said nothing. Olu
came out of the kitchen door, and was followed by Bukola
both carrying bowls of different sizes.

'What are you two talking about?' Olu asked.

'Tonje is just telling me that he's a novelist,' Mike replied.

'An aspiring novelist,' I chipped in before either Olu or
Bukola could speak.

'Has he told you that he's practically giving birth to a new novelistic genre?' Bukola asked wickedly.

'Oh, how novel!' Mike mused in return.

'Yes, the whole thing is so novel — I predict it's going to amount to a disaster!' Bukola said.

'Never mind the seeming antagonism between these two — they'll only use you to revise themselves, and even you in the process,' Olu said between gritted teeth. She still looked dangerously vengeful and somehow irritated at the way Bukola had invited me to their place tonight and the effect wasn't lost on Bukola and I.

'I'm serious Michael,' Bukola said — addressing Mike by name for the first time, and it was just like Bukola to adopt the formal rather than the informal version of the name: 'Look! how can you lump together a whole range of disparate bodies in a cultural orgy of violence our native son describes as ethnobiography?' Bukola queried.

We all laughed, while I said, 'She's only worried about how she's going to feature in the whole story. Olu, can you remember the famous tale of one Ekiti girl at Elizabethan Island in Port-City who cried herself hoarse whenever she was fed sausages and chips instead of pounded yam and melon soup?'

'Well you see that's my point precisely. The whole thing is going to be so libellous whatever little money you make from the sale of your sacrilegious story would simply disappear into paying damages to x, y and z!' Bukola rallied.

'I thought the whole thing was going to be so bad, he wouldn't even find a publisher for it in the first place?' Mike stated.

'Assuming he does,' Bukola retorted: 'How would he get away with all that prying into other people's private life?'

'Sounds sort of historicist to me,' Mike replied cautiously.

'Historicizing who?' Bukola screamed: 'I mean whatever this boy knows about me and my family don't exactly qualify as material to be placed before a cosmic audience — does it?'

'Not if you view things from a micro as well as macro levels — I suppose. But look, I shouldn't be holding brief for Tonje. After all the griot himself is here to speak for himself,' Mike stated.

'Our story is only a departure in the sense that it tries to narrate the peculiar experience of a people — a much misunderstood, maligned people. I can't and I'm not even calling the story mine, because it's not,' I said.

But it was Mike who asked the quintessential question again: 'Misunderstood and maligned by who?' he asked.

'By a whole range of forces from within and from without.'

'I guess you'll have to be more specific than that.' Mike stated again.

'You'll have to read the story then ... Ours is...!'

'Hey Tunji, food is ready,' Olu announced before I could finish: 'Some people are here to eat, and not on a spying mission you know,' Olu said wickedly.

We moved to the table where Olu continued to play the vengeful host. She introduced the menu to Mike, and asked if he was an adventurous eater. Ignoring Bukola and I completely, she filled Mike's plate with a mouth-watering quantity of fish pepper-soup, placing the basket of bread in front of Mike. Bukola got the hint, and moved to fill the remaining three empty plates. Mike grinned and asked if Olu would rather be served by her younger sister:

'I've told you to avoid clichés tonight but you seem determined not to heed my warning. Well, I hereby declare myself cleared and absolved, and I'm no longer responsible for any error of commission or ommission ...' Olu went on to say.

'She's speaking in riddles again,' Bukola said before Olu could finish.

We sat in total silence, Bukola and I watching Mike's first intake of the pepperish soup keenly. If we expected him to burn there and then we were sorely disappointed. After several mouthfulls, Mike declared that the soup was delicious: 'Thank you Mike. At least those that came to watch a murder plot can now return home disappointed,' Olu stated simply.

Mike looked from Bukola to me before asking what that was. 'Oh! Never mind,' Olu replied: 'Let's just say that we also have our own clichés and stereotypes, and the culprits in this particular instance certainly know themselves.'

'What is she talking about?' Mike asked, his gaze on Bukola.

'I wish I knew. That's the case with kinship — it often insists that because we're entwined — we must rip each other in the thigh! As I said, some of us have been endowed by a most capricious existential logic to build bridges, and can only hope to lead others away from their fixations and myopia,' Bukola opined.

It is extremely doubtful whether Bukola thought she could get away with that line with her sister, but hasn't it been said that defense is really the best form of attack? Mike's mouth dropped, and I lowered my face into my bowl of soup, expecting fireworks. Olu laughed mirthlessly and said: 'Riddle me this riddle! Bridges, Existentialism, Myopia — wonders indeed would never end. Who do you think you are, Bukola?'

In return Bukola lowered her face into her bowl of soup. Olu sighed heavily, muttering under her breath. Mike scrutinised the faces around the table and finally said: 'Do you guys always talk in riddles?'

'O Leviticus, O Jeremiah, O Jean-Paul-Satre!' Bukola said and we all laughed.

'So it was all a bluff?' Mike asked without prevarication.

'And the real heroes of every society are the artists who have…!'

'Oh! No!' Bukola screamed before I could finish.

'But you said it yourself Mike — didn't you?'

'Said what?' Mike asked truly confused.

'That it was all a bluff!' I repeated stupidly.

'Look Mike, this boy has been looking for a way of concluding his sacrilegious tale without sounding contrived. But if you ask me that's really the most contrived interior monologue the world would ever know,' Bukola reiterated.

'I warned you Mike. I told you not to contribute too much to whatever these two are on about. Now you've contributed, without knowing it of course, the befitting conclusion to the tale of our time,' Olu chipped in.

'I would feel better if any of you would tell me what I've contributed and to what,' Mike stated sounding quite exasperated.

'Never mind Mike,' I said, trying to reassure the flustered

Home Office functionary: 'It really doesn't matter. Like colonialism, it was all a bluff — one big bluff. The other task remains how to win people — our people — back, from that fanaticism of the mind which has driven many men to war over a matter of belief!'

Olu explained the matter to Mike more calmly: 'You see Mike, the story is as old as our phenomenal entry into the so called modern world. The story with which these two are grappling revolves around a reflexive irony — it incarnates a profound paradox. My mother, back home in Baluba, and our aspiring griot here are upholding a thesis which is the task of our sister here to invalidate.'

'I've got no such task!' Bukola protested before Olu could finish: 'I just don't like the idea of this boy leading a people into any false conciousness.'

'So where is the difference?' Olu asked again: 'Anyway as I was saying Mike, the thesis is that colonialism was one big bluff, and Tunji could you please supply the other parts of the dogma?'

'Don't snigger Olu — it doesn't become you! We've got a battle on our hands and you know it. I'm suppose to belong to the angry generation...'

'Oh! I beg your pardon Mike. That's another aspect of the hypothesis that you haven't heard about — the artlessness of the angry generation!' Olu said before I could finish.

'And who are those?' Mike asked.

Bukola laughed mirthlessly: 'Yes! Yes! Yes! I agree with that aspect of the thesis. There's indeed a generation of anger driven artists in our midst, and the history of their anger just like the history of laughter would be extremely interesting if ever written.'

'You're losing me again,' Mike complained: 'Now what's she on about?' he asked Olu.

'It's part of the restructuring or piecing together of the tale that you don't lose your art just because the subject matter fills you with rage. Then you'll be treating the symptom, as they say, instead of the disease — the lie instead of the bluff! Am I right Tunji?'

'Yooou! Youu are right — righteous! — elder sister', I said between guffaws. Bukola had bottled up into a posture we knew so well. 'The Portrait of the Artist as an Angry Young Man' is Bukola's entirely, and she plays the fool as well as the serious critic. Asked to explain where all the artistic imperatives have gone in his *magnum opus,* the writer replies simply 'I'm just too angry!'

'Well, my question is if you declare colonialism a bluff — what then is neo-colonialism?' Mike asked genuinely.

'A bigger bluff!' Bukola replied, and we all laughed.

'Yes, you're right Bukola if colonialism was all bluff, this contemporary beast is a far bigger bluff! The world is — was — and would always be a Masquerade — A Dancing Masquerade.

Three

'No offense intended, but if I were a liberated woman and playing it straight I might be calling myself 'Something-Smith-Ridgeway-Anything' today,' Mike said for the umpteenth time.

'You mean to say that the Bishop Andrew Smith and his wife — who are credited with bringing the Christian faith into Aiyeru and other parts of Baluba — were your grandparents?' Bukola asked again.

'Yes, they were my mother's parents, and like them, my own parents also served in Baluba — of course on another side of the over-analysed tripartite colonial structure.'

'And which arm would that be?' I asked.

'The administration. My father was a District Officer. He left. Baluba at the dawn of independence — a dissatisfied man,' Mike stated.

'Why dissastisfied?' Olu asked.

'It's a long story really, and as Tonje says, it's really a case of crocodiles eating their own eggs.'

'Oh! That's perfect! Just perfect! So we're into Baluban proverbs already — are we? Mike, I suggest that you submit yourself for a psychic examination and a most doubtful but possible restoration after this encounter. It's only fair that your superiors as well as inferiors know what they're dealing with. This whole point about how you got here and what you're doing here — I mean inside this dingy flat — has always disturbed me. Now are you going to announce that the love of niggers — or if you prefer the colonised! — runs in your immediate and extended family?' Bukola sniggered.

'I wouldn't put it in those strong terms. But, you're probably right. When my maternal grandparents died, their one wish was to be buried in Baluba. Of course, that wish was denied them for many reasons. My father and mother met each other in Baluba, just as my father's parents were completing a

137

posting in the RBC or Royal Baluba Company.'

Open mouthed to say the least, it was Bukola who rounded with: 'Perfect again. Can you now see, Omo-Aiyeru, why that ancestor you often berate describes history as a nightmare from which he is trying to wake?'

'I believe I can. So what you're saying really is that your entire ancestral tree revolves around the colonial enterprise?' I asked.

'Yes, the big-bluff — I'm afraid' Mike stated matter-of-factly: 'You should meet my parents — especially my father before he dies — and he might die any moment from now.'

'Why are you so sure he might die anytime soon?' Olu asked

'First let me say that knowing him as I do he would support your thesis of the big bluff, and would also share in your belief or description of the world as a masquerade — A Dancing Masquerade!'

'Why?' Bukola asked looking angry.

'Well, just as my grandfather saw through evolutionary Darwinism and proclaimed survival of the fittest a philosophical retrograde...!'

'Oh! Have you been reading Bishop Smith's memoir?' I asked stupidly.

'Don't be stupid Tonje! The original — I mean, the handwritten copy is in my parent's house! But, as I was saying, my father fell out with the colonial administration because he disagreed totally with the plan to supplant democracy in Baluba,' Mike rounded.

'What do you mean supplant?' Olu asked.

'A memo from the Colonial Governor-General landed on my father's desk informing him that Baluba had been zoned, for continuity sake. One zone would be in charge of government, another would take care of the economy, and yet another would be responsible for diplomacy and so on and so forth. This decision, the memo explained was reached after extensive study of the behaviour and attitude toward the colonial administration's policies of the different groups inhabiting the different zones of Baluba. The first general election was about to take place and what that amounted to was that if the group mostly favoured to take over the government didn't win, the colonial government would help somehow. My father and the other District Officers were implored to supply ideas as to how that could be easily achieved,' Mike explained lengthily.

'You mean supply ideas about how the elections could be rigged?' I asked.

'Yes and No!' Mike replied.

'What do you mean yes and no?' Olu asked aggitated.

Mike was in pain, and his agony was palpable: 'The first part of the plan was not to rig outrightly,' Mike said at last. 'Facilities — in terms of ideas and resources would be placed here and there — albeit in favour of the favoured! To put it mildly, everything would be done to ensure that the playing field wasn't level between the different groups contesting and vying for political control of the infant Baluban nation,' Mike responded.

'But that would be patently undemocratic,' Bukola screamed.

'Precisely, and my father wrote to the GG telling him just that!'

'And then what happened?' Olu wanted to know.

'The rest as they say is history. He was fighting a losing battle and he knew it. He wrote in his memo to the GG that the colonial adminstration was about to lose the only redeeming aspect left of the colonial enterprise — the opportunity to leave Baluba with a future that would be the sole choice of her citizen — after centuries of exploitation and plunder!'

'And what happened?'

'When his protest became unbearably loud, a plan was hatched to silence him.'

'But how?'

'An early retirement was considered, but dropped immediately. He wasn't even close to the official age of retirement, so he was offered the position of Governor-General in another colony — albeit an inconsequential one — or at least, one considered to be so in the colonial imagination.'

'And?'

'He refused. He wrote and wrote — to everyone and anyone who cared to listen. Unfortunately for him the people he meant to help were the ones who took him less seriously to his chagrin — but to the amusement and pleasure of the colonial administration.'

'You mean our emergent, purely technocratic elites?' Bukola sighed heavily.

'Our redeemers who changed their minds!' Olu echoed.

'Our very own redeemers whose minds are eternally blurred,' Bukola replied.

'Yes!' Mike said in affirmation: 'They were too absorbed in the battle to become this and that — and failed to see that as far as the colonial administration was concerned, everyone's role in the scheme of things had been preternaturally predetermined!' Mike concluded.

Four

The journey to Mike's parents promises to live up to its billings! We are as excited as we are apprehensive. The dinner last night was almost ruined by all the talks. But Finally, at 2 am, Olu announced that it wasn't safe for anyone to leave the flat anymore. Bukola moved into Olu's room, so that Mike and I could share her room. The decision was reached that the following day being Saturday would be ideal to visit Mike's parents. The one hundred and fifty miles would be more picturesque if we went by coach, and the decision was reached that we do just that.

'Talking about living-ancestors Omo-Aiyeru,' Bukola said in the morning: 'I'm convinced that Paul and Mary Ridgeway are one.'

Not that any of us had been able to think of anything else but Mike and his ancestors. Aiyeru of the days of Bishop Andrew Smith occupied my own veritable horizon. I dreamt that the Bishop Smith who also fell out with his superiors was hanged by a screeching mob — not in Aiyeru or any other part of Baluba but in his own country. He was first given a hero's welcome — an official motorcade, retinue of welcoming, flag-waving, frantic dancers accompanied the bishop to his official residence. But the dissatisfied section of the Pharisees and Sadducees were not amused. They plotted silently. Allegations ranging from efforts to civilise the natives to sympathies for their primitive cultures were levied at Bishop Smith. Before a kangaroo court of the Sanhedrin or Council of Elders, the cacophony of noise finally reached crescendo level, as the mob screamed: 'crucify him! Crucify him! Away with him!' I woke up, sweating profusely as the Bishop hung from a tree. When I went back to sleep, the scene changed to the road to Damascus conversion of Paul Ridgeway, or to be more precise how a wicked District Officer totally unsympathetic to any aspect of native culture — suppressing them and jailing their practitioners — metamorphosed into the proverbial sympathiser wailing more than the bereaved. No particular deity or *orisa* could be said to be singularly responsible for Paul's conversion. Some say it was the battle of wits between him and the *Alagemo* that did it. Others claim it was Jakuta that claimed him, asking him with passionate entreaties: 'Paul why are you persecuting me?' Others said, 'if like Paul, you have witnessed the hanging of Sango, how can you partake everafter in ridiculing the king that did not hang?' Whatever it was, Paul moved swiftly from a believer in the univocality of his own cultural mooring to a tolerant multi-culturalist — a move that set him on a perilous head-on collision course with his kind. When told that a zealous or over-zealous DO was persecuting the acolytes of this or that *orisa*, Paul came resolutely and unfalteringly to the rescue. His move between natives and aliens alike became more purposeful. He preached understanding and tolerance. He practised kindness and humility. To the natives, it became common knowledge that '*orisa* had claimed Paul.' To the aliens, besides the numerous allegations of having gone-out-of-his-mind; gone native or gone berserk, Paul Ridgeway became a stumbling block — and one of offence!

Inside the coach, Bukola sat next to me, while Mike and Olu occupied the seat behind us.

'Did you warn your parents that we were coming? Bukola asked.

'No! It's absolutely unnecessary,' Mike replied.

'You mean that we will budge in on them just like that?' Olu asked.

'I thought that would be best. My mother likes surprises, and father doesn't fuss about protocols either,' Mike said again.

'That's settled then,' Olu said satisfied.

'No, it's not!' Bukola screamed beside me: 'The picture this guy is trying to paint is of the exotic Baluban — 'the perfect song' as they say! No we are not. We are 'the abused stereotype.' I insist that we get off this coach and phone your parents at the next stop, and arrange the whole thing in a modern and civilised manner!'

Preoccupied with different thoughts, Olu and I didn't even smile. But Mike laughed wildly, and called Bukola crazy.

'Yes, you're right, she's crazy, and she has been for I don't know how long,' Olu said agreeing with Mike.

'Well, if you guys', meaning Olu and I, 'would rather present yourselves as uncouth Balubans, I guess I can't stop you butt...'

'Spare us the preaching Bukola. We have a right to present ourselves the way we want. If Mike says it's alright what else do you want?' Olu asked.

'I ask that we present ourselves with a bit of decorum,' Bukola insisted.

'And has it occurred to you that one man's decorum could be another man's major irritant?' Olu asked.

Entering the Ridgeways' residence was like stepping back in time. It was as if the entire rain forest had been transported to the place, and you could be forgiven for thinking that a baboon or his signifying brother, the orang-utan might surprise you at any moment.

'The rain forest didn't just fall on us, we fell on the rain-forest!' Bukola cried as we entered the Ridgeways' garden.

We met Paul Ridgeway precisely where Mike said we might find him at this time of the day. He was attending to every plant in the sumptuous garden as if nothing else mattered. The acacia shrub complemented the gum Arabic, while the medicinal *péregún* or evergreen tree bestowed a talismanic quality on the pockets of roses and hibiscuses. Paul stood before each plant like a diviner. He spun round as he heard his son call him father. The look on his face showed that we could have walked past him without his notice if Mike hadn't hailed. Tall, pencil-like, like his son, Paul Ridgeway's eyes brightened the moment he saw his son and the three of us.

'Let me guess' he said without prevarication, 'you have come to announce to me and your mother that you've found a Baluban girl to marry.' We all laughed wildly as if he had cracked the wildest joke we've ever heard.

'Now let's see which of the two sisters it could be,' Paul continued as if in meditation. He scrutinised Olu and Bukola quizzically and threw up his arms in despair: 'My world! They're both beautiful and you must be spoilt for choice son.'

'Father, these are my friends. Olu, Bukola and Tonje are Balubans as you've rightly guessed, and they're here to see you and mother before...'

'Before what?' Bukola snapped before Mike could finish. 'I'm telling you again that I have always distrusted this fellow's intentions, and Tunji...'

'Oh, she definitely can't be the one then. She's too strong a character for Mike!' Paul said. 'But come and meet your mother first. She's somewhere in the house, and I'm sure she'll be pleased to meet your friends. Now tell me, what are the three of you doing in my country — as if I need to ask. We looted your land, didn't we? And to make matters worse, left you with a neo-colonial condition that wasn't even of your own making?'

'We have contributed a lot to that too. Just look at the pathetic figures we call our leaders! The one that took over the reigns of power a moment ago is not as intelligent as the previous one, and the previous one wasn't intelligent at all!' Olu responded.

'How's the torture chamber, my boy?' Paul asked Mike as we approached the entrance to the house.

'Still torturing innocent souls! I met Olu there and that's what led to all this,' Mike replied.

'Now which one is Olu again? Oh! I see — she's the older one. You must have been lucky it wasn't the youngest of the pair. I don't see that one allowing you to advance beyond officialdom. How do you deal with our sardonic monument my dear?' Paul asked Bukola, as we stepped into the living-room.

Bukola laughed in return and said: 'I'm a student sir, and as long as my fees are paid duly, my stay is rather automatic.'

'That's what we like — don't we, Mike? The education industry is another monument to... Oh, Tunji I can see why that attracted you straight-away. Unfortunately, it's found a resting place where it never belongs — it's at this very moment resting at the largest monument to robbery the world would ever know — our museum!' Paul said as he caught me entranced before a giant portrait of a brass figure.

'But what is it?' I asked stupidly, still entranced.

'That's an *Edan*, and it's the soul of your culture. The fact that it isn't resting where it should be at the moment means that your culture is soulless — to put it mildly!' Paul replied matter-of-factly.

'And what really happened to it?' Olu asked.

'You're that social anthropologist — I suppose?' Paul asked in return.

'Yes — I inherited the ordeal from my mother,' Olu replied.

'It's an ordeal alright,' Paul said in agreement. 'You've got a lot to do if you really want to help your people. That *Edan* is just one-minute example. It was stolen from the royal palace by the son of the Oba forty years ago, and sold to one of our university professors — that tribe made a tiny fortune calling themselves collectors. During their yearly vacation, they brought down their loot which they sold to our monument here or others on the continent. Anyway I know so much about the story of this particular *Edan* because I was involved somehow. The Oba's son was caught, and taken to the court of a fellow District Officer. The elders came to me, and I agreed to speak to the DO under whose jurisdiction the matter belonged. Like many other issues, it was an exercise in futility. The prince — what a thing to call a thief! — but that's what he was, a prince-thief! — was found guilty and jailed for six months which did not prevent him from continuing his shady trade in antiquity after his release! Mike would take you to the basement after lunch, and you can examine my photo library. It would take you about a week just to view them. Anything you see standing physically in this room or any other part of the house were things that my wife and I commissioned this or that wood carver to make for us. More than ninety-five percent of those in my photographs on the other hand, are resting right now where they shouldn't be!' Paul concluded.

Just then, Mary Ridgeway's stocky frame filled the doorway

at the other end of the living-room. Mike held his mother's hand tenderly as if he was about to introduce a priced performer to an expectant audience. Dressed in a maxi batik, Mary continued to smile and the son held her close to himself — her head resting just beneath his armpit.

'Mother — these are my friends Tonje, Bukola and Olu,' Mike said.

'How are you my children? Mike has told me so much about the three of you; the femme-terrible, the social anthropologist and the novelist!' Mary said pointing at each of us in turn.

'Don't believe anything he says,' Bukola replied quickly.

'Yes, he told me that you're a difficult one to figure out. But how could he? Poor child! All he knows is our view of the world — and what a view that is. From the way we treat the market like an organism with a life of its own to our notion of progress!' Mary said to Bukola in particular.

'But didn't you describe the world as a market place some time ago Tonje?' Mike asked.

'True,' Mary replied her son before I could answer: 'The world is indeed a market place, and what you do in that sort of market is bargain in an imaginative, creative manner. Bargain everything — including your destiny. But how do you achieve that in our situation when prices are first rigged before being fixed?'

'Well, back home we are already counting the high-cost of not-living! Our markets have grown from centres of intense activities to one inhabited by somnambulists,' Bukola replied.

'That's right,' Paul echoed. 'For people like you who probably grew up knowing what a Baluban market used to be, that can only be sad. It's our notion of progress as Mary said. Our ancestors pandered to the notion of the world as a dancing masquerade — if you want to see it you don't stand in one place! — when they trampled the earth. But their successors — obsessed with a most treacherous wealth that accrued from the colonial adventure — would have none of that. For them, the position of the individual within the cosmic system must be fixed, even when that position is first rigged — as Mary says — before being fixed!'

Mary Ridgeway walked to the centre of the living-room leaving her son leaning on the doorpost.

'Paul!' Mary said: 'Can you remember my first day as a housewife — in a Baluban market?'

'Oh! How can I forget that!' Paul said laughing hysterically.

'What happened?' Mike asked anxiously.

'Nothing disastrous really. But it's an experience you can never forget. I was not brought up, you see, to associate creativity with marketing. For me, a market was where you went with your lips tightly sealed, and big frown on your face. But the sight that confronted me was one of boisterous gaiety and I couldn't deal with that. You could spend a whole day in that market — buy nothing! — and still return home happy and fulfilled,' Mary replied.

'But how?' Mike asked again.

'Quite easy son — quite easy,' Mary quipped: 'The buyers as well as the sellers are there — or so it seems — to enjoy themselves. They're both seasoned participants in the art of buying and selling. Isn't it true Paul that buying or selling in that market was an art.'

'You're right — an art of the most intense sublimity,' Paul responded.

Olu laughed ruefully, and said: 'Our grandmother used to describe the ordered-noise of the market as food for the soul; you ignore it only during that fraction-of-a-moment you want to select an item!'

'That's right. You're there to enjoy yourself the rest of the time. From the creativity of an *Alárìnjó* to that of an *Apidán* group or even the antics of the proverbial every-woman's husband — you can't be bored,' I chorused.

'Proverbial-every-what?' Mike asked with squinted eyes, and we all laughed.

'Yes, you never call a madman mad,' Paul announced: 'The women simply address him as 'my husband'!'

'And that works?'

'Like magic,' Mary replied. 'My husband why are you doing this or that to me... my husband could you fetch me this or that, and so on and so forth.'

147

'And what about mad-women?'

'If the woman was married and had children before she became mad, then you simply call her Mama this or that — the most popular ones are the mothers of twins — they're hailed as Mama-Ibeji, meaning the mother of twins all the time,' Olu replied.

Five

The decision that I interview/ask Paul and Mary Ridgeway some pertinent questions concerning their life in Baluba — in short about the Baluban past and present — was reached just before lunch. They consented straight-away, and we agreed that after lunch the interview would commence under their favourite acacia tree.

Lunch consisted of black eyed beans — cleaned hurriedly by Olu and Bukola the moment Paul and Mary said that *moinmoin* cooked with red palm-oil rather than vegetable oil — was their favourite Baluban dish. The duo's attempt under Mary's watchful eyes and supervision was a roaring success. Rice and fish stew completed the menu, and belching loudly at the end of the meal, Paul declared that the sweet wine distilled from the palm-tree would have brought him nearer home.

Paul took Mike and I on a guided examination of his incredible collection of photographs. I said to Paul: 'The transatlantic slave trade, fratricidal and internecine wars, colonialism, neocolonialism and above all, the rush to modernize the 'erstwhile relative pseudo-scientific' outlook of Baluban cultures have been allotted varying degrees of blame for the precarious Baluban present. The questions that any casual observer of the contemporay Baluban scene might ask concerning the Baluban past and present, are legion. Before the era of multinational companies and a tripartite not-so-new world-order or disorder conspired to create a consumerist socio-cultural, political and economic psyche in the Baluban — what was? Long before colonialism and its over-analysed tripartite organs, (viz: the notorious trading companies, arrogant and insensitive administrators, and last but not least, the many peddlers of spiritual acclimatization) armed with their univocal version of reductive and deductive reasoning, desecrated and trampled over the resources, minds and bodies of the Balubans — what was? Given the internal conflicts with which the Baluban societies of those days were riddled, were they in any position to present a coherent front against the rapacious that confronted them from without? Finally, is it not a truism that even during the infamous slave trade, the Carthaginian might have proposed, but was it not the Baluban that disposed?'

Paul starred at me long and hard, and replied cautiously: 'There are no straightforward answers to those questions. Of course, different organs of the over-analysed tripartite organs as you've described them, are responsible for different historical and contemporary malaise. For example, the creation of thinkers who perceived the cultural and religious outlook of their forebears as riddled with superstition and inimical to the fancy footwork that the television set, glossy magazines and cinemas from across the Carthaginian world brought to their living-rooms, I would regard as a collective responsibility. We were all responsible — in my opinion — for the creation of the liberal or so-called liberated Baluban thinkers whose minds were agitated by the Carthaginian image of the pop-eyed Baluban chanting 'bwana, bwana, me see iron-horse!' Our ideological opponents assisted a great deal in creating the political left who maintained/retained an uncritical dialectical outlook.'

'But father,' Mike interjected, 'are these analyses not necessarily simplistic? Are we saying that there are no people within these tripartite structures who thought differently — who tried to do things differently? Where is your own position for example, in all these?'

'You're probably right Mike. On both sides of the great divide, a few indeed thought differently. We could have had true partnership instead of treachery — brotherhood instead of avarice. Let me read to both of you what a young missionary wrote in the middle of the nineteenth century, when he ascended a lofty granite boulder and looked down upon the Baluban city of Aiyerugba. In his book *In Baluba's Forest and Jungle: Six Years Among the Balubans*, he wrote: 'What I saw disabused my mind of the many errors in regard to Baluba. The city extends along the Ogun for nearly six miles and has a population approximately 200,000... instead of being lazy, naked savages, living on the spontaneous productions of the earth, they were dressed and were industrious... (providing) everything that their physical comfort required. The men were builders, blacksmiths, iron-smelters, carpenters, calabash-carvers, weavers, basket-makers, hat-makers, traders, barbers, tanners, tailors, farmers, and workers in leather and morocco... they made razors, swords, knives, hoes, billhooks, axes, arrow-head, stirrups... women most diligently follow the pursuits which custom has allotted to them. They spin, weave, trade, cook, and dye cotton fabrics. They also make soap, dyes, palm-oil, nut-oil, all the native earthenware, and many other things used in the country.' When I arrived in Baluba a century later, I found a very similar situation. All the crafts the missionary listed were very active. Baluban towns were industrious. They were bursting with activities. In Aiyerugba we lived opposite a blacksmith's workshop. All day long half a dozen craftsmen were busy producing hoes, cutlasses and other farm tools. They were even forging the pellets for short guns by hand! They tended to beat in a steady rhythm, like musicians creating a 'groove'. From time to time they interrupted their work for a brief spell to recite oriki on what you might call a 'talking anvil'. Then you knew that some important men were walking down Ibokun road. Looking down into the Abolubode compound from my back verandah, I could see a woman weaving aso oke on a vertical loom. Within five minutes walk, I came to an alaro's compound, with huge dying pots standing in an open courtyard. Yarn, kijipa or adire were hanging up to dry in the sun. There were many alaros and many aladires in Aiyerugba and the cloth market was a feast for the eye. A large variety of aso oke and adire was on sale. A speciality of Aiyerugba women was the heavy men's sleeping cloth: a kind of toga in stripes of different shades of indigo — woven, of course, from thick handspun cotton. I still have some of these clothes in my possession: after forty years they have neither faded nor worn thin! Adire Eleko was so common that you thought nothing of cutting up the most refined 'Ibadadun' or 'Eyepe' pattern to make yourself a shirt. Intellectually one knew, even then, that

151

these crafts could not survive the onslaught of Western industrial products. But you could not really imagine such a situation, because these arts were so alive. There was leather work and refined embroidery. There was even a brass caster who lived down the road. Only the great Baluban tradition of woodcarving had ceased to exist. Obas and Chiefs no longer commissioned carved pillars, and the Olorisa were too poor to commission *ere*. Many of the old carvers had become carpenters, and they now made wonderfully, inventive and elaborate chairs for the Obas: a new art form! Another new art form was cement sculpture: lions, elephants, and occasionally soldiers placed on the balconies or arched gates of 'Brazilian' houses. In many respects, Aiyeru, Aiyerugba, and Aiyederu were fairly traditional towns. Of course there were inroads into the culture: each town had its motor park with its noise and, if you like 'vulgarity,' and its new professions or tout, *mekaniki* and vulcaniser. But even the motor park had their own culture: the tails boards of lorries were usually painted with proverbial proverbs and images ('*Iwalewa*' or character is beauty, could often be read at the back of a truck!) In those days the truck drivers would cleverly manipulate their motor horns (rubber balls at the end of a shiny horn), in order to address potential customers. They could actually 'talk' on these new instruments and inform people that they were about to depart for Port-city or Ebaodan. Often enough, when I lived in Aiyerugba, they woke me up at three or four o'clock in the morning. People liked night travelling in those days, because the roads were safe and one could reach Port-city in time for a full day's business activity. To cater for the travellers, clusters of restaurants grew up around the motor park. A 'modern' development, because in a traditional town there was obviously no need for a restaurant. But these little restaurants were wonderful places: you could eat pounded yam with *egusi* or okro — superbly cooked. The women would compete with each other. You sat in a simple wooden shack, with a corrugated iron roof. The tables, in those days were scrubbed until the wood became white, and exposed its markings. The entrepreneurs would also sell palm-wine or, if you preferred, sent out for Star beer. Some motor parks had a

152

nationwide reputation for the quality of their cuisine and the availability of bush meat. Travelling to Igboko or further East, I would invariably stop at Oke for a meal. Even architecturally, Baluban towns in the fifties would not have been all that different from the Aiyerugba the Reverend saw a hundred years earliér. He would have seen a sprinkling of Brazilian houses, blending harmoniously into the townscape of sprawling mud compounds... Hun! A Baluban town used to be a maze of large rectangular mud compounds. The size of these compounds depended on the terrain: in the landscape of Aiyederu province they tended to be huge. In the hilly areas of Ekiti, they were more compact...'

Part Four

Where then is the nigger's
Home?

In Paris, Brixton, Kingston,
Rome?

Here?
Or in Heaven?

What crime
His dark
Dividing
Skin is hiding?

What guilt
Now drives him
On?

Will exile never
End?
(Edward Brathwaite, *Rights of Passage*)

He who increases
Knowledge increases
Sorrow.
(Ecclesiastes 1:18)

6. The Return

One

Night fell while Paul recounted the epic tale of Baluban Renaissance and woes. Mary held Paul's left hand tightly as if to help him through his painful remembrance. The temperature fell along with the falling night, and Mary helped Paul slowly to his feet. Bukola proferred a hand which Paul took gracefully and gratefully: 'Stop treating me like a monument,' Paul complained.

'You're not! You're an ancestor — a living-ancestor,' Bukola replied firmly.

The look of bewilderment that registered on Paul's face lasted just a fraction of a second. The Baluban concept of *Ìwà* or character — *Sùúrù* or patience, to which you could add *Ewà* or beauty, all received crucial equivocation at that moment. For a people who value their unity as much as their diversity, the Baluban recognises that there are different kinds of *Ìwà* and people respect that, but 'if you want to be respected as a king, as a priest, as a diviner, then you have to have *Sùúrù*... *Sùúrù* is a form of pragmatism, and the gregarious imbibers of this view of the world know better than to kill a fly with a sledgehammer. Hence they readily admit that

> *It is with calculated patience*
> *That one kills the sandfly*
> *That lands on a man's scrotum!*

'What did you say Tunji?' Olu asked as we approached the entrance to the living-room.

'I was just thinking about this and that,' I replied.

'We're all thinking about this and that. But you were mumbling something about calculated patience — or am I imagining things?'

'No,' I replied. 'I was remembering the age-old saying of our people that it's with calculated patience that one kills the sandfly that lands on a man's scrotum!'

The look on Olu's face changed from one of bewilderment to a sudden lightheartedness: 'You know I'm still worried about you,' she said finally.

'What was that Tunji?' Bukola asked.

'I mumbled a prayer, and elder sister here says she's worried about me,' I said.

'Was it a prayer then that you mumbled or a curse?' Bukola asked again.

'Depends on what you mean then by a prayer. To me, it is a prayer, and one which our people have said from time immemorial' I said in reply.

'Then spit it out, and let's examine what you really said within the parameters of this multicultural setting — your curse or your prayer!' Bukola replied.

It is with calculated patience
That one kills the sandfly
That lands on a man's scrotum!

Paul chuckled and Mary giggled hysterically. Mike looked bewildered, but it was Paul that said:

'Oh! And I rather like the one with the mosquito too. You know that's a being — I mean the mosquito — who has never been accorded its due regard in the liberation struggle of your people. Take it from me as someone who should know that if not for the female anopheles, the colonialist wouldn't have left you at all. But then as I was saying — the concept of patience is encapsulated in what your forebears say about the mosquito that lands on a man's scrotum. Try killing it with a sledge-hammer — and the signifying thing would simply and regally resume its flight, and you break at least one or even the pair in the sack you set out to protect!' Paul said and roared with laughter.

We all laughed in spite of ourselves, and it was quite clear that each person laughed for a different reason. A moment of sober reflection followed, as we assumed different positions in the living-room of the Ridgeways.

'Well, it's the story of life — of existence,' Mary responded to her husband's summation.

'But how?' Mike asked.

'The Baluban socio-cultural psyche is replete with such tales. Think about it Mike — is it not a lame-duck fly or mosquito that lands on whatever that you can kill with a sledgehammer? I mean, an agile one wouldn't wait for the hammer anyway. So the saying is really an altruism — if you refuse to hearken the result as has been established is that you inflict irreparable damage on at least one or...!'

'Please stop mother! I think we've got the picture,' Mike interrupted the mother before she could finish, and we all laughed again.

'Hey! Don't be so sensitive, otherwise how can you survive the festival of abuse?' Olu said to Mike in particular.

'The festival of what?' Mike exclaimed.

'Yes, the festival of abuse,' Mary replied: 'Paul you've got to tell the children what your fellow District Officer did to stop the festival of abuse.'

'*Odun-Elegba*, it is called. When this particular DO heard that a week had been set aside when you could literally say anything — no matter how lewd! — to anyone — be it your father, mother or even the king himself he thought that the time had come to end the barbaric practise,' Paul explained.

'And he did?' Mike asked.

'To some extent,' Paul replied. 'But you see our people's mistake has always been this drive towards univocality instead of polyphony. It's a philosophical starting point that the Baluban has always being able to resolve and transcend — even anticipate.'

'Very well put,' Mary said in response to her husband.

'But you haven't answered my question,' Mike screamed at his mother and father: 'Did the DO succeed in putting an end to the festival or not?'

'Yes he did or so he thought! The imperial might was on his side you see. The Balubans were more bemused than angry. Like every other aspect of their socio-cultural mooring that has received one form of abuse or another from the colonialists, they could only marvel at the zeal with which every organ of the colonial machine pursued its own version of a most vitriolic univocality,' Paul proffered.

'So they simply gave up — capitulated once again?' Mike asked.

My mind raced back to the scene in my mother's kitchen at Elizabethan Island in Port-City many years ago — when she described my willingness to apologise as weakness — and I said: 'The point that you're missing Mike, is that confrontation is not always strength. There are several other options — equally potent — that one could fall back on before confrontation.'

'Including capitulation!' Mike replied.

'Yes, including capitulation,' I readily agreed. 'But if as Paul says, you're more bemused than angry — what do you do? You've been taught from cradle to respect strangers — no matter how vicious — she's or he's got something to contribute to your socio-cultural mooring — even if that which she or he brings there and then appears negative.'

'Then what is evil?' Mary asked, and we all saw that she meant to help.

'Precisely Ma,' I said in response: 'what is evil? Again, we've got a complex response. In any remonstrable matter between two parties or individuals — one or even both might behave in an evil manner for a plethora range of reasons — drive for popularity, bigger profit or simply the well known primordial bestial instinct that is in everyman! The reasons are legion. But that does not mean that the one who behaves in such a manner is the devil! The matter is so simple, the imperial might obfuscated it.'

'Yes, in their bid or non-bid to locate the concept of evil among your people!' Mary said again.

'Precisely. So our god of fate — enigmatic, signifying and at times capricious — became for them Lucifer or Satan. Some have located in that translation a bid — a deliberate one — to demonise Baluban culture and religion. Yet others — less temperamental or less piqued — have said that it was a case of ignorance rather than oppression. Like the anti-racist racism theory with which we've grappled — it's neither here nor there,' Olu replied.

'Absolutely,' and it was Paul again that supplied the quintessential encapsulator: 'But of course, a lot of harm was done through ignorance. A friend of mine used to point out that the Colonial Education Ordinance started with the sentence: 'Education is an instrument of change.' The implication is clear. Education was not a means of widening people's horizon. It was not attempting to build on what was there already. It was a matter of discarding everything you had, suspending any belief you held, disowning every kind of wisdom you ever held and embracing wholesale and without adaptation — somebody else's lifestyle. So it was the education system that deliberately helped to destroy the fabric of Baluban society. I will give you just one example — many of the school teachers and clerks who were personal friends of mine, could not understand why I spent so much time with Sango worshippers. They could not see the beauty of the dances or the poetry of the music. They could not read the beauty in the faces of these magnificent people. They simply said: 'Sango does not exist.' I said: 'why not?' 'Because you can't prove it.' I said: 'Can you prove the existence of the Christian God?' To them one is 'superstition,' the other 'truth'. They measured both with a different yardstick,' Paul rounded.

'It's our optical delusion. In one realm you're prepared to suspend disbelief — in the other you keep it intact,' Bukola observed.

'One set of mythology was taught as fact. Baluban mythology was denounced as some backward, heathenish, even evil superstition. Nobody ever explained the difference between 'truth' and 'fact.' Nobody ever attempted to find the common ground between the religions. After I'd been accused of having 'gone native' — a human being who has dropped all his standards, who has gone 'to seed,' become mentally derelict — you could say that I became a missionary of some sort myself. I became the object of much prejudice. That didn't

160

bother me, but it was sad that there were even a few Balubans who felt the same! Anyway, in my own little attempt at a counter-discourse of the imagination, I went around — gave lectures and assisted wherever I could to call Balubans back to themselves. I once told a class of Baluban kids that the Baluba people had their own version of the Biblical myth of 'Paradise Lost.' Every single child knew the Baluban myth that said: 'Once upon a time the sky was very low down, and when people were hungry they could simply cut off a piece of sky and eat it. For a long time everybody obeyed this rule, until one day a greedy woman cut off a huge piece of sky. She could not finish it, and even her husband and her children and all the relatives could not finish it. The entire village ate of this huge piece of sky. When they could not finish it, the woman had to throw the remains on the rubbish heap. The sky felt deeply hurt and removed itself from human reach. Since then, human beings must plant to eat!' But the Western trained Baluban teacher felt offended. He thought I was undermining his authority and putting funny ideas into the children's head. The children, who had younger minds and were less prejudiced responded with curiosity and enthusiasm. I pointed out that the story in many respects compared favourably with the Biblical one. That the idea of course, is the same. That once life was better and easier. That man was closer to God. But through man's own fault, and disobedience, hardship was brought into life. The difference lies in the image of God. The Biblical God is all powerful, cantankerous and self-righteous. He is in fact taking revenge. In the Baluban story — God is *vulnerable*. He can be hurt. The vice that has brought the misfortune upon mankind is not so much *disobedience* but *greed*. The story is perfectly applicable to Baluba society today. It is above all greed that has created even greater distance to God that has ultimately destroyed Baluba society,' Paul concluded.

Two

And yet we multiplied knowledge. Knowledge of whom we are and where we are — where we're from and where we're going. The journey back to capital city was far less argumentative — less contentious. We sat as before. Bukola held the palm of my right hand in hers, and Mike and Olu sat together. The vice which has brought misfortune upon man-of-a-kind is not so much *disobedience* but *greed* — we've all learnt.

'But what about the other fear — fear of failure which has driven many to this and that?' Bukola asked.

'Ah ah!' I replied: 'The 'Other' fear is not even your own fear — rather it's a fear created in you and I by forces whose sole intention is to turn us into what we're not — what we cannot be!'

Three

The turn of the keys at Olu's and Bukola's made Mike and I realise that we've been with the two sisters for the past seventy two hours.

'You can both leave now if that's what you want' — Bukola said as if reading my thoughts.

'Is that the Other fear?' I responded and Olu asked what that was.

'Never mind,' I said: 'Let's just say that this girl and I have been philosophising on the three evils of our contemporary existence — disobedience, greed and fear!'

Olu turned the keys and pushed the main door open. We all felt in varying degrees the fatigue of the two and a half hours journey — indeed of the past seventy two hours — and all the talking and activities at the Ridgeways. I collapsed into one of the easy chairs and Bukola fell on top of me. I held her close to me — more to cushion the impact of her deliberate fall than anything else. She steadied herself and I shifted to make more room for her on the easy chair. Olu disappeared swiftly to her room and Mike went to Olu's and Bukola's collection of Compact Discs. He squinted at the endless rows of discs and selected a disc finally. The striking note of one of our favourite spirituals soon floated in the air — filling the room:

> Hush... Hush...
> Somebody's calling my name,
> Hush... Hush...
> Somebody's calling my name,
> Oh, my Lord, Oh, Lord,
> What shall I do?

I felt and tickled Bukola's scalp through her short hair, and she closed her eyes. I must have dosed off, but when I opened my eyes — I found Bukola's head resting peacefully on my chest. I looked at her shapely mouth and was overcome with emotions. A realisation that I never knew was there over-powered me and I struggled to shake it off. Mike wasn't in the living-room any longer, but the disc of spirituals was still playing other tunes.

'No Mike! I don't think it's right!'

Bukola and I heard the unambiguous sound at the same time, and it came resolutely from Olu's room.

'Oh, my God!' Bukola exclaimed, and I helped her gently to her feet. She blinked hard and shook her head vigorously to regain full consciousness. We were thinking the same thoughts, and she gave in without any resistance. I picked her topcoat as well as mine, and we shut the door of the flat gently behind us.

'To which of the three debilitating emotions — *Disobedience! Greed! Fear!* — are you reponding?' I asked Bukola.

Bukola spoke into the mouthpiece softly and irritably: 'What is wrong is wrong,' she proclaimed with banality. It was my turn to giggle into the mouthpiece. 'What sacrilegious noise is that?' she asked, still irritated.

'Your seeming understanding of all that is right and wrong about human nature. Remember what Paul said about separating *fact* from *truth*? Look Bukola, I know how you feel, but we must learn to respect other people's feelings too you know!' I said.

'Oh! That is brilliant — just brilliant. So I'm the irrational one now? Is that what you're saying — you sacrilegious griot!' Bukola screamed and I was glad that she was several miles away, and couldn't pelt me with missiles as she often does.

'Calm down,' I said into the mouthpiece, knowing that with Bukola that was like dousing a raging inferno.

'No, I'm calm — I'm so calm I feel like killing somebody! In fact, I've got to kill somebody — and it should be you native son! I know that this thing is not right, and you keep telling me to calm down,' Bukola rallied.

Mike resigned from the Home Office a week later. 'My position

164

there is no longer tenable,' he said to me after dinner with the two sisters.

'So what are you going to do now?' I asked.

'I don't know, but I'm trying to figure out what the future holds for me,' he said, before adding in a half-plea, half-soliloquizing manner: 'would you guys take me to Baluba?'

A palpable silence descended on the living-room. Olu starred into space, and I felt utterly transmuted. Bukola's shapely mouth curled into a familiar serpentine position and I thought she was about to curse the life out of Mike. But Mike looked determined — defiant — smiling capriciously.

'Are you sure you're doing the right thing Mike?' Bukola asked at last.

'YESSSSSSS!!!' Mike said deeply. 'But I need your approval — anything less than total acceptance wouldn't do.'

Olu stood up and approached Mike cautiously. She held his head which in her standing position came to rest just above her navel.

'Oh! Isn't that sweet!' Bukola mused sonorously: 'But I've got a better idea' Bukola announced further, and we all laughed.

'Okay shoot — we're all ears,' I said.

'Mike! why don't you just withdraw your resignation before it's too late and we can rearrange the whole thing. My candid view is that you will probably be of more use to the revolution if you remain within the system here. You'll be the Baluban man — I mean pointman! — at the Home Office where you will issue — on instruction, of course — permanent residence permits to both deserving and un-deserving Balubans. We'll call it the triumph of sexpionage over espionage. Think of it — how many of your people already have permanent insights into the Baluban system? Even our cabinet — I understand...'

'Hey! Hey! Take it easy,' I said: 'We've got the point but give us a chance to examine the pros and cons of one proposition before you bring in another. As bride-price — the idea appears sound to me! But I forsee a problem!'

'Which is?' Eyes blazing, Bukola asked.

'You guys are sick,' Olu interjected before I could answer: 'You're sicker than I ever thought. Whose bride-price are you arranging if I may ask?'

'Elder sister — with due respect — I suggest that you keep well out of this. This is a matter of utmost national interest and security, and nothing in my view could be more important since the days of Chiefs selling their people for the trinkets ...'

'I agree with you again homeboy, but what problem do you forsee?' Bukola asked again.

'The problem of counter-insurgency,' I stated flatly.

'On whose part?' Bukola asked again.

But Mike smiled and said: 'I see your point Tunji. But you have nothing to fear from me. You've helped me — all of you — far more than you know. The world as you've often said is a masquerade — *a dancing masquerade* — if you want to see it, you don't — you just can't — stand in one place. The vast majority of us have stood in one place — in our pursuit of what my father describes as a most vitriolic univocality in place of polyphony — for too long. The big-bluff — is one other thing that you helped me with. You don't know how much of a bluff that torture chamber where I've been earning my keeps represents. Call me a crossover — or a passover — if you like, but something tells me not to stand in one place if I want to see or know the world in its polyphonic, melodious beauty.'

Paul and Mary cut regal postures as they listened intently to their son. In her pious — utterly blissful resignation to the dictates of enigmatic fate — Mary or *Moremi* complemented the outlook of the Paul whose conversion took place long ago on the way to Ilubu. Mike behaved like Oluorogbo and an unmistakeable passover lamb. In that sense — and only in that peculiar sense alone — can you forgive him for being so blissfully capricious in his new-found state of assumed fulfilment. He walked the garden of his parents' home hand in hand with Olu, and it was as if he wouldn't let her out of his sight forever. Bukola sat back in one of the many cane chairs that adored the Ridgeways' garden — eyes glued to her sister's back. Mary's eyes were trained on Bukola, and I in turn studied Mary's face.

Finally, it was Paul who had been observing the three of us that broke the silence and said: 'So what do you children think of all this?'

'You know I wasn't even thinking about those two in the garden!' Mary said: 'But you two would make a wonderful couple,' she slipped in casually, bringing Bukola and I back to body terrestrial.

'What was that?' Bukola asked eyes blazing.

'Mother here just said that you and I would make a wonderful couple,' I replied mischieviously.

'Meaning that you've finally found that somebody's daughter you've been fantasizing about for so long! No! I hate to disagree with you but you're wrong there mother. I've known this boy all my life and I can assure you that I don't find him appealing in that sense at all,' Bukola replied.

'Well, you see mother, there you have it straight from the horse's snort. Our liberated Baluban princess lives in hate: She would use me when and if she needs me, and that's where the matter ends!' I said.

But Paul continued to smile. It was Mary that echoed his thoughts: 'Does anything remind you of a certain defiant girl whom you once stooped to conquer?' she asked her bemused husband.

'Yes and No!' Paul replied calmly. 'There are differences as well as similarities all right, but what is happening here is the post-celestial outcome of affirmative action!'

'What do you mean?' Mary asked confused.

'You see the world — this world which is like a furious Masquerade — A Dancing Masquerade — has turned full circle in our life time, and we have hardly noticed it. In our bid — I say *our*, even though I've never acquiesced in that bid! — to impose and streamline, we've confused the *Order of Things*. And I'm not speaking about the old fashion cliché of the hunter and the hunted here, but about a new, probably post-celestial training in repression — repression of deep human desire borne out of fear. So instead of re-affirming or rediscovering that order we assume that we're affirming in inaction! That's my view!' Paul rounded and rested his glittering eyes on Bukola. Bukola's countenance fell and she smiled. But as she began to stutter, Paul turned to me and said: 'And you my boy — are you not scared silly of what our *femme terrible* might do to you should you give words to those thoughts locked in your chest!' It was a half-statement, half-question and we all laughed at Paul.

'But you've lost the plot there homeboy,' Bukola screamed again. 'Oluorogbo is dead and buried. We're talking about a living Olu now, and this one happens to be the child of my mother! The former is a myth, the latter a reality.'

'Yes, daughter-of-a-bird that...'

'Cut out the cliché Tunji,' Bukola screamed again before I could finish.

'Okay' I said: 'Since you want it straight I'll give it to you straight. Can't you see the marked resemblance in the evolving creative scenario? It's the gods themselves that are in control here.'

As images of crossing and re-crossing, the notorious Middle-Passage bubbled in our hearts — it was clear that each of us was imprisoned in different thoughts. But when this remembrance is over — I said to myself — I sincerely hope that I'll be able to piece the entire story together. Inside the giant Air-bus taking us back to Baluba, it was impossible to dream. A huge radar map showed the gradual advancement of the giant bus towards Baluban climes. The name itself was presumptuous and I swallowed hard to contain it — a bus in the air! Paul sat next to me, while Bukola and Mary huddled together and conversed animatedly about the gods alone know what. Olu held Mike's hand tightly like you would a prized captive. The task of securing a Baluban visa for Paul and Mary wasn't an easy one — but one which Paul had led us to anticipate. The moment the official at the Baluban embassy beheld the names — he disappeared swifly and returned with a superior officer within five minutes.

'Hell-O! Mr. Ridgeway!' he said into the microphone on his

side of the cubicle. 'Silly how we keep borrowing all the master's tropes without any creative adaptation,' Olu whispered furiously into Mike ears, but it was loud enough for several people to hear. Paul returned the man's greetings politely and the man asked Paul and Mary to come with him into another room. They reemerged thirty minutes later saying the man would have to clarify matters with his superiors in Port-City before he can grant them visas. Bukola was incensed and she screamed her indignation at the entire vicious machine: 'It's okay for you to issue permanent residence permits to so-called prospectors and directors of trading companies whose ancestors have exploited our land and people for more than two centuries, but not to people who actually assisted us in the process of decolonisation!' Bukola screamed. Mike was dejected as he assisted me in dragging Bukola out of the embassy. Moving swiftly in Port-city, it was Bukola's mother that broke the vicious machine. Wedding invitations arrived from Baluba announcing the solemnisation of the relationship between Olubunmi Osanyin Jr and Michael Ridgeway. The visas were granted soon afterwards.

The Air-bus touched down at the airport in Port-City just before dawn. Like the fairy tale it was meant to be — the saga has merely just begun!

Epilogue

When you make a vow to God, do not
Delay to pay it;
For He has no pleasure in fools.
Pay what you have vowed.
It is better not to vow than to vow and
Not pay.
(Ecclesiastes 5:4-5)

Everyone pledged!
Each one pledged!
We all pledged!
My neighbour pledged a huge goat.
My brother pledged a fattened calf.
But Olurounbi alone pledged her offspring — her only
offspring. To heal a world — Olurounbi pledged — her only
child!

Our tale is old. Our tale is as old as the coming of Ifa into our
world. You see — we are talking about parameters —
parameters of friendship. When Ifa came to the world, he
wanted to have a slave to work on his farm. Simple matter. So
they bought one for him in the market. Ifa sent him to cut
grass on his farm. But as the slave raised his arm to cut the
grass, he noticed that he was about to cut the grass that cures
fever. He cried — son of Atunda cried — 'I cannot cut this
grass — it is too useful!' But the second kind of grass he was
about to cut was the grass that cures headache. He refused to
destroy this too. The third leaf — precious thing! — was the
one that cures stomach-ache. Then the slave-king said: 'No, no
I can never destroy such important leaves.' The moment Ifa —

170

Lord of intrigues — heard this — he asked his slave — who was none other than Osanyin — to tell him about the useful herbs. There were so many of these — so many that Ifa decided that Osanyin should stay close to him so he could teach him the virtues and uses of plants, leaves and herbs.

So — that is it! That's the meaning of the name Osanyin-bunmi — stay close to me Osanyin so that you can teach me the virtue of things!

But as the spectre of generations rose to embrace him, Mike discovered that he had found something sweet. Ah! Moroun-todun — the Orange-fish! In trance and in body celestial — Mike, Olu, Bukola and Tunji entered Banana-Bottom. But the spectre of generations rose again. This time it was Maami-Agba — in the company of Paul and Mary Ridgeway and the Ekiti witch of primordial remembrance. They came briefly and enacted the Dance of the Forest. We watched. We prayed. We moved — movingly. Paul became a masquerade — chanting 'if a woman confronts Orò — Orò would swallow her up!' Maami-Agba and Mary called his bluff and we all laughed. But the Ekiti-witch was aloof — indignant! Ah! But this world is a Masquerade — A Dancing Masquerade — if you want to see it you must never stand in one place. So it was with Pakunde (close-the-door) who pronounces the oracle for Asehin Bokin of Iseyin — 'Son-of-a-sieve, who drinks bad water from the very day he ascended his father's throne.'

But — you see — since he had become king — none of his wives had given birth. They consulted Ifá — and Ifá told them that he should go and sacrifice to his father. The Asehin made his sacrifice — but the father — signifying orangutan! rejected the blasted thing.

Then, his mother told him that his father — the one who begot him — was not from these shores — he was not even a human being!

She said: 'One day when I went to the farm to fetch firewood — there was a certain animal who resembled a human being. He forced me to have intercourse with him. Then I used a trick. I split open a tree with my axe, and asked

171

the gorilla to put his penis inside. But when he put his penis into the cleft — I pulled out the axe. His penis was caught and he died.'

'This is why your father now refuses the sacrifice. The one you're sacrificing to is not the one who begot you.'

'Some people in this town would remember the Orò (gorilla) who died in a tree. It is that same animal who begot you upon me.'

When the Asehin heard this — he went to the place in the forest. He found the bones of the animal and placed them in a coffin. Then he killed the ram.

When they carried the dead body into the town — they were singing:

> Close the doors
> Orò is coming
> The son is taking his father.
> All you landlords
> Close the doors
> The son is bringing
> His father home.
> Orò is coming!

They swung it through the air. Then the people in the town said: 'Truly this is a dead person speaking.'

So you see — Paul cried and laughed — strong guttural laughter:

> The son is bringing
> His father home!

But the spectre rose again — and it was Bukola's mother. Bukola's mother went to Esinmerin and asked — she asked on behalf of her generation — sacrilegious nincompoops! — for help. The goddess said to Bukola's mother — she would reveal the secret of the enemy provided she would agree to sacrifice her son — her son-in-law! Bukola's mother agreed and she was told how the enemy would be overcome:

When you make a vow — do not
Delay to pay it!

Bukola's mother went to fulfil her obligation. Her only son-in-law had to be sacrificed.

Close the doors
Orò is coming
The son is taking his father.
All you landlords
Close the doors
The son is bringing
His father home.
Orò is coming!

Ah! This world is truly a **Masquerade — A Dancing Masquerade!**

Glossary and Notes

1. Bean-soup is the husband, yam-flour is the wife
   Let's sing the praise of the cowhide
   The saviour of our stomachs!
2. Fried plantain
3. Christians, Muslims or Idol-worshippers
4. A policeman's wife can never give birth to a good child, if she doesn't deliver a cudgel — she's bound to beget a baton!
5. A bird so-called because of its cry
6. Cloth sellers' stalls
7. Sellers of chinaware
8. Remove yourself to that corner and examine it!
   If you're satisfied, please pay
   If you're not, just drop it
   Afterall, its only a piece of the white folks' discarded ornament!
9. what's the cloth seller's business wielding a stick!
10. Aileru Kubadi! The famous load-carrier clad in iron!
11. Cursed be your great-great-grandfather!
12. Home, Home!
    Home in heaven!
    Father has gone home!
    Straight home, straight home!
13. I dreamt, oh, I dreamt
    I dreamt that I was wearing a crown of money
    I dreamt, Oh, how I dreamt
    I dreamt that I was clad in a high-chief's regalia
    The day that I depart these climes
    The mount of redemption is where I'll love to be taken!
14. Kajogbola has been transformed into the blazing sun
    Burning with severe intensity
    Onikoyi has been transformed into the hot sun
    The heat is quite intense!

174

15. The centre of the market is where we're heading
    People of the market disappear!
16. Eyes bulging like palm-nut
    Belly button equally bulging and covered-up
17. Eyes bulging like palm-nut
    Belly button equally bulging and covered-up
    He's been made the king of cows
    Their house is just over there
    Their compound is just over there
    The doors to their house are as low as those of a rat's
    house
    Their father is just over there
    Their children are right before your eyes!
18. A child begotten by Ogun
    must possess Ogun's mannerisms
19. Cut it well! One must not surpass the other.

15. The nature of the things it wants, we feed it.
    People of the market disappear
    ... ones having the patience
    fetis b. The red die-baking and covered in
    17. Experience the bribe how...
    Belly big man equally walking and covered
    He's been inside the king's cave
    Their home is a place of three
    Birth ... opportunities over there
    He does, so their house are as long as there ... with
    house
    Their respect is just over there
    Their children are held before your yeet
16. A child is eaten by Ogun
    muse possess Ogun's magnet songs
19. Curry well One muse not support the of ...